Hot and

CW01085930

Seven Erotic Short Stories
and Hung, and Know How to Handle It

~B.J. Scott~

~Male Love~

It is beautiful, it is fine, it is the noblest form of affection. That it should be so, the world does not understand. The world mocks at it, though there is nothing unnatural about it. It is that deep, spiritual affection that is as pure as it is perfect. So often feared, it has been called, "The Love that dare not speak its name."

~Oscar Wilde~

B.J. Scott   1

Beau to Beau Books
Celebrations of Male Love

     History is written by the victors. That which society does not want known is omitted. Such is the history of Male Love, which has been revered and prevalent in societies from the earliest times of record. Beau to Beau fictional stories of Male Love are written with sincerity and passion, to hopefully inspire gay men to enjoy their lives to the fullest, without shame, which is deservedly theirs to be realized. Shame is not the gay man's to be borne. Shame is the lot of the ignorant!

     Among the Greeks, Male Love did more than dare speak its name; it fairly shouted it from the rooftops. It was one of the fundamental traditions of Greek life, one practiced and enjoyed to the fullest. Indeed, it was a social must which no poet, no philosopher, no artist disdained to explore. It was discussed in public as a matter of course and included in the reflections of the greatest minds.

With Love,

B. J.

Table of Contents

Erotic Scenes

Clive has dreamed of working in film for as long as he can remember, and after years of bit parts and minor roles in off-off-Broadway plays, he has finally arrived to star in his first motion picture. Clive's agent and producer welcomes Clive to live in his home with him while he is shooting his film, and Clive is impressed by the lavish lifestyle of his mentor and cannot wait to be a part of this lifestyle that is enjoyed by the rich and famous. Clive's agent assures Clive that everything he has ever wanted can be his if he works hard and, more importantly, if he makes the right connections while he is here in Hollywood. When Clive begins to explore the monstrosity of a house that belongs to his agent, he begins to wonder who his agent's connections really are, and he also begins to wonder what exactly is expected of him as an actor in his movie debut.

Clive had always been somewhat of a loose cannon, and it was the mystique that seemed to surround him that made him sexy. Everyone liked Clive Owens, especially Clive Owens. Clive had watched as many of his friends had settled down as the years passed, but he simply was not ready. "Maybe when I am in my forties. Maybe then I will be tired of the singles scene, but not now, not yet."

Clive had wanted to work in film for as long as he could remember, and after years of bit parts and minor roles in off-off-Broadway plays, he had finally gotten his big break. Clive had flown to Los Angeles immediately after receiving the call from his agent.

"Clive, you made it." Clive gave his agent, Sebastian, a hug when they met up with each other in the airport.

"Damn, Sebastian, I thought you said you were in your fifties."

Sebastian was very quick to correct Clive. "I said mid forties, young blood, and out here I can look as young as I choose." Sebastian patted his cheeks to show off his latest nip and tuck. "The best plastic surgeons in the world are right here in Los Angeles, California, my friend. Well, ready to get a taste of the good life?"

"Lead the way," Clive said.

Sebastian was very likeable, and not at all what Clive had expected. Clive had expected some hotshot producer, but Sebastian seemed like an ordinary guy. I sure hope he knows what he's doing, Clive thought. He has my career in his hands.

"Here we are," Sebastian said, opening the door to an awaiting limousine.

"Don't tell me this is yours. It is rented, right?"

"No. It is all mine, Clive. My last film was a mega hit. Did you see it?"

"I'm afraid I missed 'Ladies in Waiting'," Clive said, with a grin.

"Well, Clive, what's your pleasure?" Sebastian asked, opening the bar in his limousine.

"Something light. Gotta watch my waist."

"Yes, you do, Clive," Sebastian agreed, and poured them both a drink.

After a twenty minute drive on the freeway, the limo driver pulled into a gated property, and Clive could not believe his eyes. "This is your house, mansion, estate?"

Sebastian noticed the look in Clive's eyes and he knew for sure that he had found himself a winner, if he had had any doubt before now. "All of the above, Clive, but only after working my rear end off for many years. You are in the right business and in the right city to get everything you have ever wanted, Clive. Believe me, you are going to be a star, but it does not happen overnight. Remember that."

Clive had heard only a fraction of what Sebastian had just said. His eyes were fixed on the monstrosity that was Sebastian's home.

"Come on in, Clive," Sebastian said, opening the door to his palatial estate.

"Wow!"

Sebastian had Clive's things brought in while Clive stared at the double staircase that seemed never ending in its ascent.

"Sebastian, how in the world did you do all of this?"

"Well, Clive, a lot of hard work, a little luck, and connections. Connections can be your best friend out here in Tinsel Town, and your fastest rise to the skies."

Clive noted the serious look in Sebastian's eyes when he talked about connections, and he wondered who Sebastian's connections really were. I'll bet Sebastian knows the really big players in this city, and well beyond this city, also.

"Well, grab a suitcase, Clive, and I will take you up to your suite."

Clive picked up one of the two bags that he had brought with him and followed Sebastian up the long curvy staircase to his suite. Sebastian had not said "room". Sebastian had very clearly said the word "suite."

At the top of the staircase, the hallway was wide and as long as a runway in a major fashion show, and it led to the top of the other half of the double staircase. Clive stood for a moment looking down at the floor below them. "Wow, Sebastian." Sebastian smiled, and continued to the far end of just one side of the seemingly endless hallway.

Sebastian stopped in front of a set of double doors. When he opened the doors, Clive was even more impressed. "Well, here we are, Clive. This will be your home at least until we have finished filming, and by then you will probably have a much better place to call home than this old shack."

Clive walked into the suite of rooms that was just for him, and nearly fainted.

"This is your living area, Clive, and through these doors is your bedroom and bath. Through the doors on the other side is your closet."

Clive opened the doors to his closet and walked inside. "Damn, Sebastian. This 'closet' is the size of my living room."

Sebastian stood at the doorway of Clive's closet. "Well, Clive, not anymore. You have moved up in the world, and you will only climb even higher. I have a good feeling about your future, Clive, a very good feeling."

Clive smiled at Sebastian.

"Well, Clive, I have some business to attend to at the studio. I'll be home rather late tonight. Make yourself at home here. Enjoy the house. The refrigerator and bar are fully stocked. Help yourself."

Clive sat down in his fully furnished living room and threw his arms back. "Yes, I have finally made it," he said.

He walked down the long hallway and back down the winding staircase, down the other half of the double staircase this time, and began exploring Sebastian's house. He walked to the back of the house, a walk which seemed to take forever, and on into the kitchen. "This kitchen must make up half of the entire house." Clive slid his hand along the marble countertops. The place was spotless and beautiful.

The den next to the kitchen was where Clive found the bar. Pouring himself a drink, he looked at the very large photographs on the walls. There were paintings and portraits of Sebastian all over the room. Obviously taken when Sebastian was quite a bit younger, the portraits were very erotic, with Sebastian almost nude in several of them. At the far end of the wall there were three portraits of Sebastian with three different men. Damn, these are hot. They looked as if they had been part of an adult film. Is that how Sebastian made his money? Is Sebastian a porn star even now?

Clive decided to look around the house for more clues about Sebastian's life. He didn't find much else, at least not on this floor. There has to be a lower level in this monstrosity of a house. He had not seen any stairs that led down to a lower level, though. Oh, well, he thought. I'll look tomorrow. I'm beat.

Clive walked back upstairs to his suite and into his bedroom. He sat down on the bed. Then he noticed the bathtub that looked more like a swimming pool. It was sunken, and the water was gurgling off and on. "Cool," he said. He stripped his clothes off and stepped down into the warm inviting water. He sat down on the bottom of the tub and rested his head against the side. The massaging jets felt good, and Clive closed his eyes. It must have been close to an hour before Clive got out of the warm water and into the room sized bed. He fell asleep instantly.

Clive awoke to the unmistakable sounds of sex. Then he remembered that he had not closed the doors to his suite. There was no mistaking Sebastian's deep husky voice. Sebastian's bedroom, or suite, must be at the other end of the hall, Clive thought. He lay on his back and listened to the erotic sounds coming from just down the hall.

Sebastian's husky voice moaned, "Do me good, honey. You will like my plump ass. Lots to hold onto while you slide that hot throbbing cock of yours into my big hairy ass."

Clive knew that Sebastian was gay, but Clive wasn't sure if Sebastian knew that he was gay, too. He has probably guessed it by now, Clive thought.

Clive could hear everything that was being said as well as moaned in Sebastian's suite, and it was making him horny. Then he noticed the small flat intercom on the wall. "Oh, man," he said, and got up to make sure that the intercom was turned on. It was on. Clive turned up the volume. Then he noticed the "screen on" button and pressed it. "Damn!" When Sebastian's room came on the screen, Clive nearly fell over. "Live porn. How hot is this?"

He damned near tripped over his own feet as he hurried back to his bed, stripped his clothes off, and threw back the covers. He watched Sebastian and his young lover go at it, and would have loved to have joined them. Sebastian was one hot lover.

Clive stroked himself as he watched the erotic scene that was playing out just down the hall from him.

"You are the best, baby," Sebastian crooned. Stick that big throbbing cock of yours into my big hairy ass. I give it back real good, sweetie."

Clive watched the screen as the young man got onto the bed with Sebastian.

"Don't be shy. Come on in, Adam."

Adam might be shy, but he is definitely hung, Clive thought.

"I'm a big old bottom with a big old fat bottom," Sebastian said with a laugh. "Which is easier for you, Adam? You want me ass up or sunny side up?"

Clive watched the screen as Adam smiled at Sebastian's comment.

Sebastian turned over and stuck his big hairy butt up into the air. "Here, baby. I am well lubed and ready to be fucked." Sebastian slapped one side of his own ass hard and turned his head slightly.

Adam's thick hot dick popped easily into Sebastian, and Clive nearly came as he watched Sebastian's big hairy butt swallow it whole.

"That's my good Adam. I like it hard and rough now, son," Sebastian instructed.

Clive began pumping his own cock to the rhythm of Adam's thrusts. He closed his eyes and imagined his own cock sliding in and out of Sebastian's butt. He had never really thought of Sebastian as his type, but anyone who loved sex as much as Sebastian appeared to be loving it was definitely worth at least one fuck.

Sebastian's entire body was jiggling as he pushed back against his young lover. "Oh, yes, that's the way. You have a lot to offer this old man." Adam was beginning to grunt, and he reached underneath Sebastian and grabbed his cock. "That's the way, Adam. You know what to do. Now, hard, Adam, fuck me and pump me. That's the way."

Clive was rolling around on his bed as he stroked and pumped himself while he watched Sebastian and his lover on the screen. He wished someone was fucking him right now.

Sebastian leaned his head down onto the bed, pushing his butt even higher into the air, and forcing Adam to lean up to keep up with him. "Adam, you're fucking amazing," Sebastian moaned.

Clive watched as Sebastian came all over the bed.

"Ahhh, ohh, that's it, baby," Sebastian moaned. When Adam felt the warm cream on his hand, his body went stiff as he filled Sebastian's big hairy ass with his young cum.

Clive's own cock exploded like a fountain over his hand and spread everywhere while he watched the erotic scene.

Clive closed his eyes, and when he opened them again Sebastian had turned over and was holding Adam and kissing him passionately.

"Adam's got a nice ass," Clive said, watching the two of them suck each other's tongue.

"Mmm, you are a hot one, Adam," Sebastian crooned, pulling his young lover to him.

Sebastian began to explore between Adam's butt cheeks, and Clive waited to see what was going to happen next. "Nice and tight, Adam." Sebastian kissed Adam's cheek. "Have you ever been fucked, really fucked, Adam. Tell me the truth, now."

"No," he admitted.

"Damn," Clive said, watching. "I'll fuck you, Adam," Clive offered, as he continued to watch the screen.

Sebastian stroked Adam gently between his butt cheeks. Then he fingered him just a little. "You are a prize, Adam, worth a million." Sebastian wrapped his arms around the young man and held him while he slept.

Clive left the screen on, and fell asleep, too. When he awoke, the screen was blank and it was quiet in Sebastian's suite. He looked down at his hand around his dick. "Damn, that was hot," he said. Adam must have left sometime while I was asleep. Clive got up and pressed the off button on the screen. All he heard was the heavy snoring of Sebastian through the intercom. "Well, I can do without that," Clive said, and turned the knob to off.

Clive's big debut was today, but he did wonder about Sebastian. Was he a porn star? Did he make porn movies? Are they called adult films now? If Sebastian does make porn movies or adult films, then why am I playing the part of a straight guy in my movie debut? Or am I?

Clive prepared himself a hot bath in the big tub. The jets felt wonderful, just like they had last night.

Clive was in the kitchen when Sebastian walked in. "Ready for your big debut today, Clive?"

"I think so," he said, noticing that Sebastian was well groomed and well dressed, not at all like he was last night. "Can you tell me more about my part, Sebastian?"

"Well, Clive, you will be given a script at the studio and like I told you, there are some nude scenes. You said you were okay with that, right?"

"Sure, I'm fine with that."

Sebastian patted him on the back as he left the room. "You'll do fine, Clive. I have a good feeling about this film."

Sebastian came back into the room a few minutes later wearing a tie and a suit jacket. "Well, I'm on my way out now, Clive. The limo is waiting for you outside. Be at the studio by ten. The driver knows where to go and what to do."

"Thanks, Sebastian."

Clive dressed, and was soon on his way to the studio.

"Clive, come in. Here he is, guys. This is the man who is going to put this studio on the map." Sebastian beamed as he introduced Clive to the entire set.

Clive marveled at how business-like Sebastian was today, after what he had witnessed last night. The old man sure does like his sex.

The day was busy and exhausting for Clive, who hadn't worked much at all in the last year. Sebastian directed like a professional. Playing a straight guy who found himself caught up in a love triangle was a role that was foreign to Clive, but he had always thrived on challenges. Challenges and sex were the two things that got Clive's adrenaline pumping.

"Well, what do you think?" Sebastian asked Clive on his way out at the end of the first day of filming.

"I think it's a winner, Sebastian. I really do."

"Well, tell cook what you want for dinner when you get home. He will make you whatever you like. I will be home late tonight. Remember, Clive, help yourself to whatever you want at the house."

Clive left the studio and went back to Sebastian's house. The butler welcomed Clive, and cook asked for his dinner menu. Clive thanked them both, and then he walked up the long beautiful staircase, turned and walked down the hallway and into his suite, and plopped down on his bed. Cook asked over the intercom where Clive wanted his dinner.

"I think I'll have it in my room, if you don't mind."

"I will be right up, Mr. Clive."

"Mr. Clive," Clive said aloud. "That's good."

Clive ate his dinner alone in his room while he read his script. Seems like an okay film, nothing unusual, although he would never admit that to Sebastian. With the amount of screen time that this film was giving Clive, he would tell Sebastian that it was the best film ever made if he thought that that was what Sebastian wanted to hear. Clive still wondered what Sebastian had meant when he had told Adam last night that his virgin ass was worth a million. Everything seems like it's on the up and up to me, at least so far, he thought.

After such a long first day of filming, Clive was almost asleep when he heard what sounded like a party. He walked down the hall and looked down into the entryway, but he didn't see anything or anyone. Then he went back to his bedroom where the noise was even louder. He turned the dial on the intercom.

"In here, guys. It's all set up downstairs."

It was Sebastian again, but where was he? Clive then pressed the screen button just as he had done last night. It was dark. Then he noticed the room designation buttons to the side of the screen. Sebastian had just said something about setting up downstairs. Clive located the button for the lower level and pressed it.

Clive was shocked, but impressed, and definitely aroused by what he saw. Sebastian had a secret, a secret film studio. He *is* shooting porn. The man makes adult films. Clive looked at what he could see of the room. There were dozens of photographs of Sebastian when he was younger, and some when he was not so young. They were nude, but tasteful. Sebastian starred in his own films. Damn. Does he like the attention, or does he just like the sex?

Clive stripped off his clothes, got very comfortable in his bed, and prepared to watch tonight's show. It's going to be a good one. Clive was sure of that.

"You are the King of Porn, Sebastian. You've always been the best."

"You know it, Carl. You know it."

"So, who do you plan to make rich tonight, Sebastian?"

Sebastian stood by the walkout door of the lower level completely naked, fully erect, and waited. Then a young man, also completely naked and also fully erect, walked up behind him.

Clive looked closer at the screen. Was it Adam? No, it was someone else. Damn.

"How's my old man tonight?"

Sebastian moaned in response, as the young man held his own hard cock and slid it along Sebastian's crack.

Sebastian's head went back. "Much better now that you are here, my love."

The young man shoved his cock head into Sebastian, and then he kissed him fully and passionately as if the two of them had been lovers for a long time.

The director, Carl, spoke briefly. "That's good, guys. Keep it going. This is a hot one."

"Did you miss my cock, Sebastian?"

"Mmm, fuck me and make me your man," Sebastian moaned.

The man reached around Sebastian and held his cock with both hands while he slid his own cock into Sebastian's welcoming hole.

Clive didn't think Sebastian was acting at all. Sebastian was loving every minute of it.

"Oh, Julius, my man. Fuck me." "I am going to fuck you so hard, and then guess what I'm going to do?"

"Tell me," Sebastian moaned.

"I'm going to suck you so hard you will think your dick is going to come off."

Sebastian reared back and started fucking young Julius, and Julius held Sebastian's cock firmly in his hands. Sebastian's head was leaned back, and then he squeezed his ass as hard as he could around Julius' cock.

"Ohhh, Sebastian. You did it again." Julius put his arms around Sebastian as he filled him with his young cum.

Both men were loud with their moans and numerous other sexual sounds, and Clive lost it again and exploded all over himself.

"Sebastian, you are like fine wine," Julius moaned. "You get better with age."

"You know it, baby cakes. I'm going to hold you to your promise, though. You do remember your promise, don't you, Julius?"

Julius pulled his soft dick out of Sebastian's ass slowly so that the camera could catch it from every angle.

Julius got down on his knees in front of Sebastian, his lips at the head of Sebastian's cock, looked up at Sebastian, and licked his lips. Sebastian stroked the young man's hair and looked at him lovingly.

"Damn, this is unbelievable. No fucking wonder Sebastian is rich." Clive knew that he was talking to himself, but he didn't care. He also couldn't help but be in awe of his producer and mentor, Sebastian.

Sebastian talked seductively to his lover. "Nobody gives me head like you do, baby. Suck me dry."

Clive watched as the young man's tongue slid upward from Sebastian's balls to the head of his cock. The young man named Julius looked into Sebastian's eyes as his tongue seemed to work independently. He made slurping noises, and Sebastian closed and then opened his eyes sultrily. Julius slid his hand between Sebastian's legs and Sebastian opened them for him, and moaned. "Ahh," he moaned, as Julius grabbed Sebastian's balls and pulled Sebastian's cock into his mouth.

Clive got a good look at Sebastian's cock from this angle and thought it looked damned good for a man of his age.

Sebastian was rocking his pelvis toward his lover, and Julius always appeared to be very eager for more of Sebastian's cock. The young lover of Sebastian grabbed onto his supple hairy butt and thrust his body forward, making it look as if Sebastian might fall over him.

"Oh, baby," Sebastian moaned, and held onto his lover's head.

Sebastian began feverishly pumping his cock into his young lover's mouth, and Julius pulled

Sebastian's butt cheeks apart and then pushed them back together, again and again.

The camera focused on Sebastian's butt with the young fingertips of Julius edging nearer and nearer Sebastian's crack for several seconds, before returning to filming the expert cock sucking of Julius.

"Oh, baby, this is it. You are just too good for me to hold on any longer."

Sebastian came, and Clive was definitely convinced that he was not acting. No one can fake what that man is doing.

Sebastian moaned as he exploded into his young lover's mouth. Julius slowly pulled off of Sebastian's cock, making sure that the camera got a clear view of the cum that had shot out of Sebastian's cock.

"Okay, people, that's a wrap," the director called. Clive did not turn the screen off yet. He wanted to make sure that this was for real.

Julius continued to lick Sebastian's cock, and Sebastian was sweating as he leaned against the wall.

"Damn, you are a star, Julius."

Julius stood up and ran his tongue along Sebastian's hairy nipples before he left the room.

"Well, Sebastian, that's another hit," the director assured him.

"Mmm," Sebastian moaned.

The room darkened and things got quiet again, so Clive pressed the off button on the screen. Damn, I wouldn't mind having some of that money, he thought. Those films have got to be worth a shit load of cash.

Sebastian was looking hotter to Clive every time he saw him like this. He couldn't believe how different the old man could be at the studio during the day from the way he was here in his own home at night.

Clive was just dozing off when he heard Sebastian whistling as he came up the stairs. The whistling became softer as Sebastian turned at the top of the stairs and headed toward his suite at the end of the hallway.

The next morning Clive was tired. He wasn't used to putting in so many hours on the set. Sebastian was a ball of energy when he met Clive in the kitchen.

"Good morning, Clive. You are one damned good actor, son."

Clive drank his coffee and tried to coax his eyes to open. He couldn't believe the amount of energy that Sebastian seemed to have. Sex must energize the old man. That had to be it, though Clive had no idea how he kept up the pace.

"So, what time did you get in last night, Sebastian?"

Clive knew exactly what time Sebastian had come in, but he wanted to hear the old man say it.

"Oh, it was late, Clive. I think I average about three hours of sleep most nights, but I love my job."

Clive choked back a laugh. I'll bet you do, old man, he thought.

Clive had a hard time concentrating on his work that day, but it never showed through the camera. When the camera was on, so was Clive. He was a professional actor. There was no doubt about that. But he could not stop thinking about Sebastian, and the more he thought about him, the more he wanted to know what sex with Sebastian was like. Could it possibly be as good as it seemed to be, and appeared to be? Clive wondered if Sebastian had been filming when he was in his room with Adam just down the hall from Clive that first night. Sebastian seemed pretty sure of himself, and of his sexuality.

"Okay, Clive. Ready for the hot steamy sex scene?"

Clive thought that he was, but was also happy that it was not real. He was not interested in having sex with a woman. In the scene, Clive was naked except for his jock, and the woman wore flesh colored underwear, so the illusion certainly seemed like it was the real thing.

"Let's see now, Clive. Let's do this." Sebastian got onto the bed with Clive and the woman, and reached a beefy hand between Clive's legs. "That's better. Makes your ass look hotter." Sebastian winked at Clive, as he stepped back off of the bed. Clive was surprised that he was getting hot just thinking about the one seemingly careless swipe of Sebastian's hand. When Sebastian pressed behind his balls with two fingers, Clive felt his cock begin to grow. "That's better. One more thing."

Sebastian came back to the two of them. He reached between Clive's legs again and pulled his balls forward, making sure that Clive's hardening cock pressed against his wrist. "There. That makes a nice full shot."

Sebastian was off of the bed again, leaving Clive with a definitely full jock, his cock pushing forcefully against the tight fabric. If Sebastian was trying to get me hot, he did, Clive thought, as they resumed filming.

Clive had to admit that Sebastian definitely knew what he was doing. Getting him hot and horny made the scene very sexy. He couldn't wait until it was over so that he could jack off.

"You're hot, Clive, sexy, and you have to have it," Sebastian's sultry voice moaned, to intensify Clive's acting.

Shit, man, Clive thought. I'm going to shoot my wad if you keep talking like that.

When the day of filming was finished, Clive practically ran to the bathroom. "Oh, fuck," he said, as he was finally able to relieve his hard-on. Maybe that's why Sebastian does what he does at night. He gets so damned horny during the day that he can't take it anymore.

Sebastian was wrapping up when Clive came back out of the bathroom. "Well done today, Clive. Mind if I share your ride tonight?"

"Not at all, Sebastian."

"Tell me the truth, Clive. You think the screenplay is good?"

"I do, Sebastian. Should pull in some real dough."

"Good, let's celebrate." Sebastian smiled at his young star.

Sebastian treated Clive to a very expensive dinner that night. Clive didn't know exactly how expensive, because it was at one of those restaurants that didn't list the prices on the menu. He was impressed even more at how classy Sebastian seemed to be. If he hadn't stumbled upon Sebastian's secret life, he wouldn't have noticed the extra attention that Sebastian was giving the young waiters. The young men knew that Sebastian was a man of wealth and importance or he wouldn't be dining in that particular restaurant, but exactly what line of work the generous older man was in was unknown to them as of yet.

"Thank you, young man," he said to each waiter and server, discreetly slipping them a very generous tip.

"You never know where you will find a star, Clive."

Clive smiled. He wondered which types of movies Sebastian was looking for men to star in. It seemed to him that Sebastian made two very distinctly different types of films, each type independent of the other.

After leaving a very generous tip and having been given the usual star treatment, Sebastian walked proudly out of his favorite restaurant with his very good looking star.

"Well, Clive, join me for a drink, would you?" Sebastian offered, once they had returned to the house.

Clive sat in the den with Sebastian and accepted the offered liquored beverage. He was dying to know more about Sebastian's past, especially after seeing the naked photographs of him on the walls. Clive didn't dare mention them, though. He didn't want Sebastian to know that he had been watching him every night.

"Clive, you are a natural on the set. You aren't getting bored, are you? Do you find your role challenging enough?"

Clive felt that he suddenly needed to choose his words very carefully. What was Sebastian really asking him?

"I feel good about the part, Sebastian," he answered carefully.

"Well, you just let me know if you are desiring greater challenges. They are plentiful in this business and in this city, I can assure you."

Clive was well aware of that. Those opportunities were right here in Sebastian's basement.

"Well, Clive. I have some business to attend to. Let me know if you need or want anything. I am available to you anytime night or day."

Sebastian left the room, and Clive sat alone for awhile. Was that an invitation for Clive to join in Sebastian's other types of movies?

Clive went up to his suite and took a shower. He didn't want to miss tonight's show, and as late as it was now, the show would no doubt be starting very soon. Not taking the time to dry himself, Clive turned on the screen and pressed the button to the lower level. He was on the bed in seconds, his body already responding to what it knew was coming soon. "Damn, almost didn't make it in time," he said, as he watched the screen.

"Let's make a movie," the director said.

Clive watched as Sebastian approached a young man who looked scared out of his mind. Clive thought that Sebastian's new young man was a damned good actor. I couldn't even act that frightened, he thought.

Sebastian approached the young actor very slowly, calling him baby. When he placed his hand on the man's balls, the young man pulled away and ran out of the room.

"Well, guess I chased one away tonight, guys. Who wouldn't want some of this?" Sebastian ran his hands up and down along his body seductively.

When the young actor came back into viewing range for Clive, he was wearing a robe. Sebastian handed him a check, or at least that's what it looked like to Clive, and then he shook the young man's hand. Then he wrapped his big beefy body around the boy. "No hard feelings, sweetie. You tried it, didn't like it, and now you move on. That's life."

Clive watched as the young man left the room, but Clive's eyes were fixed on Sebastian's hard cock that had nowhere to go.

"Damn. That scared look could have made us a fortune, but I guess the young stud was really scared," Sebastian commented.

Sebastian made himself a drink, and plopped his butt down on a bar stool.

"Well, what do you think, Sebastian? Is that a wrap for the night?"

Sebastian clinked the ice in his glass. "I guess so," he replied, with a sigh.

Sebastian turned around and nearly dropped his drink. Clive had entered the room, his robe open, his hair wet, and his body glistening from the drops of water still remaining from his shower. Sebastian started to speak, but nothing came out. Clive looked hotter tonight than he did during the day, and Sebastian's cock was rising once again.

Clive walked slowly over to the bed and let the robe fall to the floor. He leaned his head back and closed his eyes. Sebastian stared at the hard nipples on Clive's young chest. The young hopeful had a damned nice dick, and Sebastian had been aching to see it and touch it and suck it since Clive had moved into his house. He wanted Clive's long cock deep inside him.

Clive opened his eyes and looked at Sebastian. He got onto the bed and spread his legs. He slapped his inner thighs, looked directly at Sebastian, and said, "See something you like?"

Sebastian wasn't sure if Clive was in his acting mode or not, but at the moment he didn't care. He set his drink down and walked over to the edge of the bed. "You have everything I like, sweetie," he said, and climbed onto the bed.

The cameras started rolling again, and Sebastian was in his element. Clive pulled Sebastian to him and licked the liquor from Sebastian's lips. Sebastian straddled him and opened Clive's mouth with his lips. Clive was hot for Sebastian. His hands grabbed the big beefy butt and Sebastian moaned. He looked down at Clive's long cock. He closed his eyes and imagined it sliding into him.

"Suck my nipples," Clive demanded, bringing Sebastian's mind back to the present.

Sebastian obediently bit and sucked the young hard erections on Clive's chest.

"Oh, that's it," Clive moaned. The cameras came closer, and the director was salivating. Clive whispered, "Suck it," and seductively urged Sebastian to take his cock.

Sebastian looked at Clive's cock and he wanted it. He leaned down and slid his long thick tongue along the hard shaft. He sucked the head, letting it pop in and out of his mouth several times, for the camera. Then he took it all, every inch of Clive's long hot cock, imagining it deep inside his big hairy ass. He let the young cock slide out of his mouth, and he looked at Clive. "I want something else, baby."

Clive knew what Sebastian wanted, but he said to his mature lover in a sensuously teasing manner, "Whatever you want is yours tonight." Clive watched as a drop of pre-cum popped out of the swollen head of Sebastian's cock.

"Fuck my big hairy ass," Sebastian demanded.

Sebastian rolled Clive onto him and spread his legs. Clive leaned up and forcefully grabbed Sebastian's legs. He fingered the big hairy hole, and the old man moaned.

"Oh, baby, don't tease this old man," he pleaded.

"You want it hard, old man?"

"As hard as you can fuck me, baby."

Clive slid his cock into Sebastian, and Sebastian's body took it all. Whatever Sebastian was doing to Clive's cock was working. The old man was good.

"Ahh," Clive moaned.

Sebastian was a damned good lover, acting or not. Sebastian met Clive's every thrust and their moans grew louder until they sounded more like growls.

"Oh, yes, fuck me hard," Sebastian shouted. Sebastian played with his own balls and pumped his cock with his hands. "No one is like you, Clive," he panted. "Keep it coming."

Sebastian's cock began shooting out burst after burst of cum. Clive growled a few more times, and then announced his own explosion. Sebastian could barely open his eyes to look at Clive.

"That's right, old man. I'm filling your hot hairy ass, and you love it."

Sebastian did love it, and so did the camera. Only inches from them for every second of this mouth-watering scene, the camera caught everything.

"Okay, people, that is definitely a wrap, and that was one fucking hot scene," Carl, the director, announced proudly.

"Ohhh," Sebastian moaned.

Clive was still holding onto Sebastian's legs, coming down from his own unbelievable climax. They were both drenched in sweat.

Clive lowered Sebastian's legs to the bed, pulled out of Sebastian's hot hairy ass, and lay down on his back beside him.

"Well, Sebastian, we've got this. We're gone now."

Sebastian waved weakly at the director and the crew. He heard the door shut, and then he looked over at Clive.

"Some acting there," Sebastian said.

"Ohh," Clive sighed. "I wasn't acting, Sebastian. You are one hot piece of ass." Clive smiled at Sebastian, but he had meant what he said.

"Shit, Clive, you're the one with the hot ass."

Clive looked around the room at the photographs of Sebastian. "You have been doing this for awhile, haven't you, Sebastian?"

"I love sex, Clive. I love hot, sweaty, stinky sex."

"I got that impression awhile back. I got that impression when I was doing you. And, just for the record, so do I, love hot sex, that is."

"Did you notice the director, Clive? He was salivating over what he thought was our expert acting."

"I barely noticed the cameras, Sebastian. The only thing I wanted was exactly what I got. So, you think you can get someone to take my place for your day film?" Clive winked at Sebastian.

"You damned right I can. That little scene that you and I just made is worth ten times the one you are working on during the day."

"You mean the one that I *was* working on during the day," Clive said, with a laugh.

"Didn't I tell you that you were going to make a fortune in this business?"

"You certainly did, Sebastian."

Clive reached over and held Sebastian's hand. The two of them looked at each other. "Let's make some movies, old man."

"You got it, my young hot cum king. Let's make some movies."

Neither of them had the strength to move yet, not after that workout, and so they slept right where they were, surrounded by the rows of nude photographs of Sebastian, the scent of raw sex lingering in the air.

Fleet Week

　　Sam and Mike love sailors, and they look
forward to Fleet Week all year long. The fine
specimens who call the sea their lady often find comfort
in the arms of men once their ships have docked and
their feet are on dry land. This year, Sam and Mike are
on the prowl again as they cruise the men in white who,
just as they, are not looking for a long term
commitment. This is their week, the week seemingly
reserved for Sam and Mike and their seafaring sex
gods. This is Fleet Week.

It was Fleet Week, the week when the Navy ships docked and the week when the entire city was filled with sailors looking for a good time. Sam and his friend, Mike, were looking for a good time, too. They loved hooking up with the men of the armed forces, be they foreign or domestic, and they especially loved the sailors. These seafaring men who had not seen land in months were horny, hungry, and had the bodies that every man dreamed of having. And, like Sam and Mike, these swords of the sea were not looking for anything serious. This was the week that Sam and Mike looked forward to all year.

Sam and Mike had had their first lust-filled adventure with a couple of naval men when they had taken a vacation to Naples, Italy, for a couple of weeks. Hooking up with sailors had all happened unexpectedly.

After visiting the tourist sites of Naples and the surrounding countryside, Sam and Mike had booked themselves a room in the Hilton in the heart of the city. They had no idea that many of Italy's finest water dogs were staying there at the same time. Sam and Mike had noticed there being more men than women in the hotel, however, on their many trips to and from their room. For the most part, though, the two fun-loving men thought nothing of it.

After spending far too much time in their room one day when the rain had decided to fall out of the clouds in buckets, Sam and Mike had become bored and decided to go out for a walk. They didn't mind the rain nearly as much as they minded being bored. This time, however, they were determined to see the "real people" of the city of Naples, not just the tourists.

The two long-time best friends grabbed their umbrellas and locked the door to their room. When the elevator opened, Sam and Mike smiled at the gorgeous hunks who were so well dressed in their crisp white uniforms. As the two friends walked through the lobby, they definitely turned the heads of the gorgeous sailor men, just as they always turned heads wherever they went. It was Sam and Mike, however, who were the ones most curious about their admirers on this vacation. These sailor men were gorgeous, fit, and they looked good enough to eat, as their butts formed perfectly shaped half moons in their well pressed uniforms.

Sam and Mike walked nonchalantly out of the Hilton, for now, anyway. They would certainly consider inviting a few of these gods of the sea up to their room a little later. There was no hurry. The day was young, and Sam and Mike knew that making their admirers wait would only make them hornier.

Sam and Mike had not walked far from the Hilton when they noticed a porn theater, and the two erotically charged men decided to see how things looked inside.

"Gotta be a great pick-up place," Mike had said.

Sam nodded, and the two best buds walked inside. It was pitch black inside the theater, so the two of them had to literally feel their way to a seat. Their hands hit more than one hard bulge as they felt their way to a couple of empty cushions. Sam and Mike could tell that the place was pretty full by the noise level, though it was difficult to distinguish words from moans.

Sam had just gotten comfortable in his seat when he felt a pair of strong hands rubbing his chest and nipples from behind. A second pair of hands came quickly across from the right and began rubbing Sam's dick through his jeans. He looked over at his friend, Mike, who he could barely see now, but what he could see was that his friend was getting the same treatment as he, and his friend was loving it.

The second pair of hands undid Sam's belt and pulled him up so that his jeans could fall to the floor. Sam's seven inch dick sprang into action at the prospect of a warm pair of lips on it, which formed quickly over the head of his eager pole, and Sam's dick was being sucked hard as if it were a straw.

As this was going on, another pair of lips began tongue fucking Sam from behind. Sam heard his friend moan and he looked over at Mike. Mike was completely naked now and Sam had no idea how many tongues and hands were in and on his friend. Mike was definitely loving the attention, but then, Sam was not complaining about the expert treatment that he was receiving, either. The sensation of having one pair of lips sucking his aching cock and a second pair of lips doing him from behind was sending Sam into total ecstasy.

As the tongue was working Sam's pulsing hole, Sam felt one of the men insert a finger into his hole, fucking him slowly as he moved his finger in and out while Sam's cock was being licked and sucked. This went on for a good fifteen minutes before Sam felt hands pulling him back down to the seat. He began to sit, but it wasn't a chair that he felt underneath him.

Sam felt the head of a cock pushing into him. Sam had always been a top, as was Mike, but Mike certainly seemed to be enjoying the life of a bottom this one time, and Sam had always had a secret desire to try being a bottom. Now was his chance.

The mushroom head of the stiff pole underneath Sam pushed through and immediately a bolt of pain shot through him, but for only a moment. The man waited a few seconds for the pain to go away, and then he pushed slowly into Sam's ass. Sam felt the pleasure flowing through him and he soon began moving up and down on the man's solid meat. He felt a pair of lips, the luscious pair of lips that had been sucking his dick up until now, suddenly remove themselves. Then Sam felt a hole sliding down onto his dick, a very tight hole, taking all of his hard cock deep inside of it, and Sam began riding a hard cock himself.

Sam was ecstatic. He had a dick in his ass and an ass sliding up and down on his cock at the same time. He could feel the eruption quickly building in his balls. The dick in his ass shot a load of cum deep into Sam's ass, and at the same time Sam blew what he estimated to be a two month supply of built-up cum into the hole that was firmly clinched around his cock.

A glance at Mike told Sam everything he needed to know about his friend. Mike was in heat. He was bucking and moaning like a crazy man. Sam and his mystery lover sat there for a full ten minutes as Sam felt the dick in his ass starting to grow smaller. He could feel the load in his ass dripping down onto the seat underneath him.

Sam then felt a pair of hands pick him up, all the way up to a standing position, as the wet hole slid off of his dick. He then felt both bodies move away from him, as he rested, holding onto the seats in front of him.

He didn't even care that he was nearly naked. Sam looked over at his friend again.

Mike was slamming his body down onto the dick underneath him, and Sam watched as Mike climaxed. He loved to watch Mike climax. Mike screamed and cried, "oh, baby, oh, fuck, oh, baby", in the same sequence over and over, until he had been drained of his last drop. It didn't matter to Mike who saw or heard him. Nothing got in the way of Mike's pleasure.

Then Sam heard his friend call out, "Fuck, I'm cumming," and Sam knew that was the end of Mike. Mike always came fast, and then he was spent for the night. The two men left Mike gasping as he held onto the chair, trying desperately to recover.

Sam and Mike never did find out who their porn theater lovers were. It was too dark to see anything. It didn't matter, anyway. The two friends pulled their jeans up, buttoned their shirts, and walked out of the theater, which was no easy feat with their weakened legs. They slowly walked back to the hotel in silence.

When the two travelers walked into the hotel lobby, one of the sailors asked, "May we join you two gentlemen this evening?"

Such politeness really wasn't necessary for a good cock suck or fuck, Sam and Mike had both thought. "Sure," Sam heard his own voice say, although he knew he needed a little time to fully recover. He didn't want to cheat his next sexy sailor man out of a good time. "Give us an hour, and then come to room 322."

"We'll be there," one of the men promised.

Mike and Sam quickly went to their room to shower. They lay on their beds awaiting their next go around, not knowing how many sailors would arrive.

Anyway, that was then, and this is now. As Sam and Mike watched this year's crop of sailors cruising the strip, they were both thinking about that time in Italy.

"Damn, those sailors were hung, Mike."

"Sure were. Don't know if the guys in the porn theater were sailors, though."

"Had to be, Mike. They smelled wonderful, and the guys at the hotel were as clean as a whistle, inside and out, if you know what I mean."

Mike grinned at his friend, and then he quickly turned his attention back to the parade of man candy as it passed by the two of them on the busy street.

It was unusually warm today, unseasonably warm, and Mike and Sam decided to see what was happening in the park. That was where it seemed that most of the men in uniform were headed. There was a slight breeze, and the air was filled with cologne and just the right amount of lust, or so it seemed to Sam and Mike.

The two best friends had not gotten very far in the park when a couple of sailors approached them.

"My friend and I were wondering if you could give us directions," one of the handsome sailors said to Sam.

"Sure," he answered.

The man handed Sam a piece of paper that had only a heart drawn on it. Sam looked at him. The man smiled. Then the man's friend took Mike by the hand, and the other sailor man grabbed Sam's hand. Sam and

Mike were quickly led to a secluded area and were once again in the arms of the men in white, those gorgeous hunks of the Navy. The two delicious naval men began to kiss Sam and Mike, and Sam and Mike melted. These arms were strong, yet gentle, their kisses filled with passion and lust. Sam moved his right hand to the back of his lover's head and began running his fingers along the man's short hair.

The kissing quickly led to a gentle rise in the four men's pants. The seafaring men turned and twisted as they tried desperately to relieve the tightness.

The four of them were so close to each other now that this could have easily become a foursome, but maybe some other time. Sam and Mike were having trouble concentrating as it was. Sam's sea god stopped kissing him and the sexy man and Sam gave each other a smile. Every time they kissed, their bodies were filled with ever increasing lust and passion.

"Mmm, give me more," the sailor said softly to Sam.

Sam continued, as he kissed his beautiful sailor with greater affection. They moaned into each other's mouths. They rubbed their bodies against each other. Oh, yes, this was what Sam needed. The sailor's hands never stopped stroking Sam's face, even as one of those hands moved down to Sam's chest.

The seductive sailor untucked Sam's shirt and the soft breeze met the warmth of the sailor's hands as they moved along Sam's chest. They both wanted more, much more, but they knew they had to be careful until they could be someplace inside, someplace far removed from the watchful eyes of some of their fellow members of the armed forces.

Many of these sex starved sailors' seagoing buddies were doing much the same things as they, but nothing was ever confessed and if asked, what happened during Fleet Week was either vehemently denied or greatly embellished amongst the members of the armed forces.

Sam's hands moved down to the sailor's pants, grabbing his butt with one hand while the other hand stroked the very full bulge in the sexy sailor's pants. The men's breaths began to grow heavier. Mike and his lover began moaning, too, as if the four of them were in a contest to outdo each other. The foursome had nearly reached the point of no return.

Not realizing the length of their stay in the park, it began to grow dark, and the four men left the park in search of a more intimate setting. They booked a hotel room, the sailors' treat, and the lusty lot, the four men looking for a good hard fuck, stepped into the elevator on their way to one of the penthouse suites.

Their pants were tight as they crowded into the elevator, desperately trying not to strip each other naked in the presence of the onlookers. The two couples had almost forgotten that they were not alone. The minute the door to the hotel suite clicked, the two couples began to ravish their partners. They pulled off their boxers, their hard cocks flying up into the air without warning. Sam grabbed his sailor's cock and his seafaring lover grabbed Sam's. As their grips became tighter and their thrusts grew faster, the four lovers' moans and gasps filled the suite.

Sam's lover flipped his body around so that his dick was in Sam's face and Sam's dick was now in the face of his sea god. They hungrily shoved each other's hard poles into their mouths, anticipating the treat that would come at the end. Sam's tongue moved expertly around the sailor's oversized cock. Taking this super sized man meat into his mouth was a challenge for Sam, but Sam had never shied from a challenge.

Once this captain of the sea was well on his way to an orgasmic peak, Sam pulled the overgrown cock from his mouth. The sailor gasped as his aching manhood was left wet and hard, but Sam's mouth had found something that it wanted just as much, if not more.

Sam dove for the sexy man's ass. The sailor's hole was so warm and tasted so good that Sam just wanted more and more of it. Thoughts of his previous sailor in Italy flooded Sam's mind and he ate hungrily.

"Don't stop," the sailor begged again and again, but Sam had no intention of stopping.

"Man, that is the best feeling in the world," he said to Sam.

Sam worked harder knowing that this was one circumnavigator who had obviously not had his ass worked quite like this before. Sam had his mouth full, so he couldn't tell the sexy sailor that he wasn't going to stop, but the man got his reassurance when Sam just kept on going, kept on going deeper and deeper, that is. Sam knew that he was bringing his seafaring fortress nearly to the point of blowing his load, but it wasn't quite time for that yet.

Sam wanted to feel that oversized sword of this sex god filling him. He had never seen such an enormous cock and Sam was determined to have it. Sam told the sailor to hold on.

"Turn back around and let me roll over," Sam ordered. Sam pulled his own pants down the rest of the way so that his ass was in the air. "Stick it in me," Sam demanded. "I have to feel that gargantuan slab of meat inside of me."

The sailor man took orders very well, and he shoved his thick pole into Sam. Sam was tight and raw inside without any lube, but Sam had been awakened to the sensations that came with being a bottom that one time in Italy and he wanted to feel that fullness again. Sam had really liked it that night, and he wanted it badly once again. With his super sized cock, this was one sailor who could really satisfy Sam's fantasy of being a bottom. The sailor stopped for a minute so that Sam could get relaxed from the fullness of his thick meat.

The sailor could tell that it was hurting Sam just a little. "You okay?" he asked.

"Fuck yeah. Do it to me, sailor boy."

The sensuous sailor began to move his hips up and down while Sam felt the thick hard cock deep inside him as it pushed against his walls. Sam thought he was going to split into two separate pieces, but very soon it began to feel good.

"Ohhh," the sailor let out. Louder and louder he moaned, just as the moans from Mike and his sailor lover became louder and louder.

Sam's lover made him feel good, all tingly inside, and he was giving him that full feeling that he remembered and now craved.

Sam grabbed his own cock to jack off, because he knew that he was about to cum. "Man, I'm cumming."

Sam could tell that the sailor was ready to shoot, too, and he wanted them to cum at the same time. Sam couldn't wait for the sailor to explode, to fill his insides with his hot cream, once again remembering that one night in Italy. Sam had been waiting for a second time with a sexy sailor for a long time now, nearly a year. The two men were both dripping with sweat as they grunted and moaned continually now.

Sam screamed out, "I can't hold on much longer. I can't stop. Damn."

The sailor man unleashed and filled Sam's insides with his hot cream. He began to fuck Sam faster and faster. It felt so much better now, Sam's cum acting as lube, and Sam pushed against his sexy sailor until his own cum shot out. The sailor began to slow down, and sadly, Sam knew that it was over at least for now. The sexy sailor let his dick slip out. It was still hard, or so it seemed to Sam, given its size.

Sam turned around so that the sailor man could lie on top of him and so that Sam could see his sexy sailor's face. The two of them lay there, saying nothing.

Mike and his lover had long since moved to the bedroom. Sam's sailor scooped him up and they moved to the other bed in the same room as Mike and his lover.

Once inside the bedroom, Sam's sexy sailor very lovingly asked, "Are you okay?"

"Hell, yeah," Sam said. He was a little surprised at the tenderness his sexy sea god had shown. But damn, that was one of the best fucks that Sam had ever had. He looked over at his friend, Mike, who was sleeping soundly in the arms of one of the country's finest.

Sam was not tired yet. He was not ready nor was he willing to see this night come to an end just yet. He was naked from the waist down, but the sailor began to quickly unbutton Sam's shirt. A little shocked at the man's stamina, Sam said, "Wha-what are you doing?"

Taking charge of his newly found bottom, the sailor put his mouth over Sam's ear. "I'm doing exactly what you want me to do."

He got that right. Sam was beginning to like being dominated. The sailor kissed him again, slower this time, but their tongues soon began fighting for domination of each other's mouth.

The sailor's lips moved to Sam's chest as he kissed his way downward. He began sucking on Sam's nipples, making him shudder with pleasure. After Sam's nipples were rock hard, the sailor bit them, nibbling them just the way that Sam liked. Sam thrust his chest forward, forcing the sailor to take more of his nipples. The sailor bit harder and harder on Sam's hard nipples. Sam knew that his nipples would be sore, but he didn't care. He loved it.

Only after Sam began to pull back did the sailor cease his sucking. He kissed Sam again, and then he began kissing Sam's naked body, moving downward until finally he found what he wanted. Sam was hard again. His dick was soon being held between the lips of his sexy seafarer. Sam moaned with ecstasy as his lover licked up and down the entirety of his shaft. He was doing it expertly. This sailor was no beginner.

Sam's sex god brought him to the edge several times before almost giving in to what Sam knew would feel so good that he was now begging for it. The sailor pulled Sam's dick out of his mouth and whispered, "Not yet. I'm not done with you."

"Ohh," Sam moaned. Just suck me off, he thought.

Instead, the sexy sailor turned Sam over onto his stomach and began kissing Sam's back all the way down to his crack. Then he began licking Sam inside his crack, sliding his tongue from top to bottom, rimming him slowly and then faster, clockwise and then counter clockwise, making Sam shudder once again with pleasure. He put one finger inside Sam and began moving it in and out of him, slowly at first, and then with greater speed. Then he put another finger in, and then another. "Ohh, fuck." Sam didn't think he was going to make it through this, but he was loving every minute. He had never been dominated quite like this. Sam had always been the dominator.

The sexy sailor took his fingers out of Sam and placed the head of his thick man meat right outside of Sam's hole. He moved it around until Sam began moving, too, as if he were trying to force it inside.

The sexy sailor suddenly jammed his cock hard and fast into Sam. Sam let out a yell. Dominating Sam once again, the sailor quickly put his hand over the screaming orifice and kept right on pushing his way inside. He didn't want Sam's screams of pleasure or pain to wake Mike and his buddy.

When Sam's sexy sailor had his entire oversized cock stuffed deep inside of him, he quickly picked up his pace and began pulling out and then thrusting back into Sam with his heavy overgrown cock, each new thrust harder and faster than the one before it. It felt good to Sam now, very good. These sailors were the best.

The two fuck buddies quickly began a rhythm of thrusting and pulling, pushing and hard fucking. Sam's sailor went faster, jack-hammering Sam. The man had more stamina than Sam, but Sam held on.

The sex starved sailor crammed his hard cock into Sam a final time as he released his full load inside of him. As soon as the sexy sailor had finished blasting what seemed to Sam to be gallons of hot cum into the depths of his being, Sam grabbed his own cock and with two quick thrusts he shot his load all over the sheets. Sam's sailor pulled his limp dick out of Sam's ass and collapsed onto the bed next to Sam.

The two of them fell asleep with their bodies intertwined. Sam smiled as he held onto his sailor man. He was determined to never miss Fleet Week.

Desperate Measures

Kicked out by yet another girlfriend, Jason desperately needs a place to stay. Not wanting to hear another lecture from his best friend, he cruises a bar where no one knows him. Hoping to find a kind older gentleman to let him crash at his place for awhile, Jason encounters something that he is not expecting, something that he fears may lead him into danger.

Jason and Randy had been good friends for longer than either could remember. They were straight best friends, though many who saw them together would have sworn that there was something there, just a little spark between them. But Jason and Randy were never like that. They didn't see that in each other. Not once during their many times together had they even considered doing anything sexual. Back when the two of them were fresh out of high school, any gay bar would have welcomed them gladly. They were the hottest looking guys, and back then they would have been the hottest twinks for some hungry sugar daddies. Whenever Jason and Randy were seen together, the moment they walked into a club or bar everyone stared, men, women, it didn't matter. The grown men would drool over the two hot young guys. But Jason and Randy were not interested in men. Jason and Randy were straight.

Now Jason and Randy were a few years older, had put on a few pounds, and had stopped getting anything waxed. These two friends had a lot in common, but one thing could be seen by anyone who looked at them. They were hairy. Their chests were hairy, their backs were hairy, their balls were hairy, and their asses were even hairier. They didn't care. They looked good. The abundance of hair looked good on these two hot guys. They looked manly, and the scent their hairy bodies gave off was all man.

The hair on Jason and Randy was dark, so it could not be missed. When they thought about it, they couldn't believe they had once been bottle blondes, or that they had waxed everything that had even a speck of hair on it, hoping to impress some woman.

B.J. Scott   48

"Shit, we look better just letting it all go," Jason admitted.

"Yeah, but we were kids then. What did we know?" Randy agreed.

Sure, the two best friends were no longer twinks, and they didn't exactly work a room full of men into an erotic frenzy like they had easily done in years past, but they still looked good enough to score, every time. But Jason and Randy scored with the ladies, even though they knew that the men were eyeing them, too.

"Ever thought of giving into one of those guys, Jason? You know they want us."

"Naw, I'm a ladies' man, Randy."

But somewhere deep inside, both Jason and Randy had thought about giving into one of their many male admirers. But neither friend would ever admit that to the other, not ever. Randy had been the first to stop adding the blonde highlights to his dark hair, and Jason had soon followed, and they had made the decision to stop waxing soon after that.

"We were beginning to look like skunks, with our black and white streaks," Jason commented. "Now we are just hot."

The two best friends were not twenty years old any longer, but they were not past their prime yet, either. With plenty of good years ahead of them, the two had filled out nicely, with big beefy cocks, big hairy balls, and butts with plenty of firm flesh for some lucky lady to grab onto.

The two best friends could still turn a man's head, and the women, well, they had had no trouble in that area at any time in their lives. Whenever they went out cruising, and they had decided long ago that they would never be too old to cruise, Jason and Randy went together, always as a pair, as they cruised the parks and the bars, and sometimes a back room or two. It was well known by those who had wanted them that if they saw one, they also wanted the other one. Jason and Randy had always hunted together, hunted for prey to lay, that is. They were always on the hunt for a nice piece of ass and the two of them could never get too much of a good thing.

But tonight Jason went alone to a bar he had never been to before. He was broke and he didn't want Randy to find out about it. He just didn't have the nerve to tell his best buddy that yet another girlfriend had kicked him out of her apartment. She had kicked him out for the same reason that all the others had kicked Jason out. Jason had been cheating on her, but this girlfriend had caught him. Always taking his friend's side, Randy had told Jason that the bitch was no good for him and he had been right, as always. Now Jason had nowhere to go. Randy would have gladly taken him in, but Jason just couldn't bear to hear yet another of Jason's lectures.

Jason felt like a fish out of water in this town and in this bar. Other than Randy, he didn't know anyone well enough to ask to take him in. Jason thought that maybe an older gentleman would offer him a place and perhaps even a few bucks. Hell, he would even promise the old man a blowjob. He was that hard up for cash at the moment. He looked around the bar hoping to find his one-time sugar daddy, but this was a whole new crowd to Jason. There were guys here, and they were definitely looking at Jason. They just weren't what Jason had expected. Then his eyes caught them. The two big beefy bears were eyeing him as if he were a side of beef. It was if they could sense the scent of fresh virginal meat. To them, Jason was a virgin. He did look the part, too. He looked innocent enough with his big blue eyes and long eyelashes. His shoulders were broad and his waist was fairly small in comparison. But somehow Jason got the feeling that it was his plump butt that the two bears were really watching and waiting for.

The two men looked hungry. Jason had seen that look of hunger before. He had seen that look of hunger in himself and in his friend Randy when the two of them were eyeing some fresh pussy. He knew that the two bears wanted to stick their big beefy tongues into his tight hole before the night was over.

"How about another?" the bartender asked, as he set a fresh beer down in front of Jason.

Jason was just about to tell the man that he could only pay for one, but the friendly bartender quickly added, "Courtesy of the two gentlemen over there."

The bartender winked at Jason and glanced in the direction of the two men.

"Shit," he thought. "What should I do now?" Jason glanced quickly at the two men and gave them a slight smile, which they interpreted as sexy shyness.

The two men smiled back, their smiles broad, as if they had just hit the jackpot. Jason hated to admit it, but he was a little aroused. His girlfriend wasn't the best lay, and Jason was horny tonight. Jason watched as one of the men placed a big beefy hand around his bulge which was also full. Jason nearly laughed at the man's obvious gesture of "look what I've got." Jason glanced away. "What am I doing?"

The two men were talking to each other, and Jason continued glancing their way every once in awhile. He tried to hear what they were saying to each other, but the noise in the bar drowned them out.

"What say, Bob?"

"I don't know, Mack. I think the man is straight. Better be careful with this one."

"A virgin, you say, Bob?"

"Yep, that's what I think."

Mack could feel his big pouch become tighter inside his jeans at the thought of taking a virgin home tonight. Bob watched his hungry friend. "Okay, tell me what's up. I know that look. You going for the straight guy?"

"That baby is going to sit down on my tower of power for about an hour or two if I have my way," Mack announced proudly.

"Could you at least pretend to be civilized, Mack?"

"Nope. Not in my nature, Bob. I belong in the wild."

"Well if you're going for him, do it already."

"I'm going, Bob. Be patient."

The big man named Mack slowly approached the unsuspecting Jason and introduced himself.

"Name's Mack," he said, and shoved his big beefy hand in front of Jason.

"Jason. Thanks for the beer."

Mack grinned. "No problem, kid." Mack straddled the bar stool next to Jason, placing his big hand on his full bulge and pulling it forward. The ride was always more fun if the guy was at least a somewhat willing partner. After a little bit of mindless chitchat, Mack motioned his friend over. "This is Bob. This young fella here is Jason." The two of them shook hands, and Bob took a seat behind his friend.

Jason was new at this and he didn't know what to say. "Are you two guys lovers?" Jason asked.

Mack's broad grin was once again spread across his face. This was going to be one hard night. This guy Jason is sweet and innocent, just like I like 'em. "Friends," he said. "Just good old friends."

Jason could feel his cheeks flush. What a stupid question, he thought.

"What brings you out here all alone, Jason? What kind of man are you looking for?"

"Oh, I'm not gay," Jason said. "I just need a place to stay for awhile. Down on my luck." Then Jason felt his entire body begin to sweat. What am I saying to these guys? I don't even know them.

Mack knew right away that he had snagged a good one tonight. "Stay with us. We're just a couple of real nice guys, you know, harmless." Mack turned and grinned at his friend, Bob. Mack wanted this hot fresh meat so badly that he could almost taste the man. He was practically salivating.

"That's very nice of you," Jason said. "But I'm not that naïve. Somehow I get the feeling that if I stay with you two, I will become your dinner or midnight snack. At any rate, I will have to put out, right?"

"Excellent, kid. Yes, you will indeed have to put out." Mack wasn't going to lie. He also knew that somewhere deep down this kid wanted to try it with a man at least once. He had seen that look before. And Mack was good, very good.

"I just broke up with my girlfriend. She kicked me out. I really just need a place for the night. I was hoping I could crash somewhere without having to have sex."

Bob laughed out loud, a big hearty laugh. Mack patted him on the leg. "Easy, Bob. Let's not frighten the lad."

Then Mack turned to Jason and looked him square in the eyes. "Sorry, buddy. I can't help you with that. Everything has a price and, of course, everything is for sale." He looked hungrily at Jason's crotch when he said the last part. "Tell you what, the offer still stands. If you change your mind before the bar closes, we'll be here."

Mack and Bob left Jason on his own after that. They knew he would be theirs soon. Jason was tempted, and Bob and Mack could always spot a young man who wanted to give it a go, as they said.

Jason was still hoping to find someone who might take pity on him. "It's just for one night," he said to at least three other guys. But he had no luck with any of them. As the night wore on, he began to think about Mack's offer. Would it really be so bad? I have always been curious? What did they plan to do? Maybe they just want me to suck them off, or maybe, maybe they want to suck me off. That would be mind blowing. My girlfriend wouldn't even try it. "Fuck it," he mumbled.

Jason went to find Mack. "Okay, what exactly do I have to do?"

"What's that?" Mack asked, as he looked up from lining up his perfect shot in the pool room.

"You know, what do I have to do....I mean, in bed? What do I have to do if I go home with you two guys?" he asked.

Mack looked at his friend, Bob. Then he turned back to Jason. "I can't speak for my friend here, but as for myself, I plan to eat your ass."

Jason just stared at the two men. He was shocked. He wouldn't have thought of that in a million years. "Sure, that's cool," Jason said, trying to wipe the look off of his face. "But you won't try sticking your cock up my ass, right?"

"Of course not," Mack promised. "Now, come on. Let's get your sweet ass home and have some fun."

Twenty minutes later Jason was standing in the living room of a beautiful home. Did this home really belong to one of these two guys? They certainly didn't look like Jason's idea of millionaires. There was a sculpture of a huge penis at one end of the living room. "You like my artwork, Jason?"

"Yeah, it's very good."

"Never would take me for the artsy type, would you?"

Jason shook his head as he stared at the unique phallic symbol. The two guys seemed at least halfway normal. Jason was well on his way to being drunk, but it was probably better that way.

"Let's get started, Jason. Show us what you got."

While Mack and Bob watched, Jason dropped his pants. He was embarrassed. He had never been naked with other men, not even with his good friend,

Randy. He was even more embarrassed about being halfway hard already. But damn, these two beefy looking guys wanted to eat his ass. Jason knew he would never get that kind of offer again. Jason immediately held his hands in front of his crotch.

"Now, don't hide the family jewels," Mack teased. Mack slid to his knees and brushed Jason's hands away. The big beefy hand grabbed Jason's cock and guided it into his mouth.

"Ohhh," Jason said. Nothing in the world had come anywhere close to feeling this good. Mack was a god to Jason now. His mouth worked Jason's cock until Jason was harder than he had ever been. He thought he was going to explode instantly, but he didn't. He held his breath. He wanted this to last forever.

Bob stood behind Jason, wrapped his arms around him, and began stroking his hairy stomach and chest with his big warm hands. Bob's fingers lightly danced over the hair covered skin of Jason's stomach and well defined chest. Jason could feel his nipples getting hard and with the occasional tweaking from Bob's fingers, Jason moaned.

Mack's warm mouth worked on Jason's shaft and cock head while his hands stroked down over Jason's full balls and down along his thighs. Jason had forgotten all about not wanting to be with a man. This kind of pleasure was not to be questioned. Two guys were doing him, and Jason didn't care.

Then he felt Bob begin to part his ass cheeks, and Jason gasped. Bob and Mack switched places. Mack was the one who had wanted to eat Jason's virginal ass, or he at least wanted to be the first man to have that pleasure.

The warm thick tongue of Mack pushed inward and along Jason's canal. It was the most amazing thing that Jason had ever experienced. The blowjob and the ass eating at the same time made Jason's legs feel like rubbery tubes. The pleasure pulsed through his entire body.

"Save me some, Mack," Bob ordered.

"I will. Be patient."

Jason didn't care who did what. He was being done, and that was all he cared about.

When Mack had Jason well lubed, he pulled his tongue out and looked at the glistening folds of Jason's virginal pucker. Then he bit lightly on Jason's ass cheeks and kissed upward along his back all the way to his earlobes. Mack had Jason's cock buried deep in his throat, and Jason hoped that Mack would slow down a little. He didn't want him to bring him off too soon. Mack was loving this. It had been a long time since he had had a virgin. Jason had the most beautiful cock he had ever deep throated, and it was the perfect fit for Mack. He could have deep throated this young stud all night long. Mack came off of Jason's cock just long enough to hear Jason's, "Ohh," and then Jason looked down to see his rock hard erection lathered in Mack's saliva. Mack looked up at the young virgin. "Let's go to the bedroom."

Not saying a word, Jason was led to the bedroom where Mack and Bob told him to get on the bed. They positioned him to their liking and took turns shoving their tongues, mouths, and hairy faces into his crack, making him writhe and squirm in pleasure.

Jason's cock oozed out a steady trickle of pre-cum and he could feel his cock glide over the bed covers. Jason squirmed more and moaned louder. "Damn," he said. And then Jason felt something different. It was cold and slippery, and it was rubbing over his asshole. Jason clenched his ass, but his well lubed canal allowed Mack's lubed up finger to slip easily past and on into him. "What, wait," Jason tried to say.

Jason felt shock and panic, and then he was quiet. Something incredible was happening inside his ass. The more Mack swirled his finger around, the better it felt. Mack spread another glob of gel into Jason's ass and the feelings of pleasure only intensified. Jason squirmed around on the bed, hoping that the finger would soon be replaced by something much bigger. Jason now wanted the very thing that he had been afraid of all this time. Jason wanted the real thing. He wanted to be fucked by a man. He squirmed more. He had to know how it felt. "Ohhh," he moaned, with every pleasurable twist and twirl of Mack's big beefy finger.

Then Jason felt something warm and spongy rub against his asshole. It felt even better than Mack's thick finger had felt. The thick cock was moving up and down along Jason's well lubed crack, over and over again, the cock head teasing Jason's wrinkled virginal folds.

"Come on, man, do him," Mack commanded.

So it was Bob's cock that was at his hole. Jason no longer cared whose cock was at his hole. He only wanted that cock to go deep inside of him.

The thick cock began to dip in and out of Jason's slippery hole. Jason had no idea this would feel so good. Every part of Jason was on fire. But he wanted more. Jason bobbed his ass up and back against Bob's invading rod until the thick cock was buried deep inside of him and Jason could feel Bob's pubes against his ass cheeks. Bob grabbed onto Jason's legs and enjoyed the moment before gently stroking Jason's hole. Jason lay there and let the feelings wash over him with each new glide of Bob's massive cock. Then Bob began to thrust harder, and Jason's pleasure intensified more and then even more.

"Fuck me," he screamed. "Fuck my hole, harder." Jason was now demanding that he be satisfied.

Jason reached underneath his own body and grabbed his cock, and he raised up on his knees. "That's it, man," he moaned, as he exhaled.

Mack was watching the entire scene, and he was so turned on by the sight of this virgin getting his first ass fuck and enjoying it so much that he knew he would not be able to wait his turn. "Hey, let me in on some of that action," he demanded. Mack pushed Jason's hand away from the cock it held and moved underneath him.

Then Jason felt his cock being taken by Mack's hungry mouth, and he thought that he would die from the pleasure. "Shit, oh fuck," he screamed. Jason's entire body was on fire. He felt nothing except for pleasure, the pleasure in his ass and the pleasure of Mack's mouth sucking his cock all the way inside of it and on down into his throat. Mack was damned good at sucking cock. He had a throat made for cock. The three men were loud as they sucked and fucked and got fucked.

Bob withdrew his cock nearly all the way from Jason's inviting ass, and then he slammed back into him hard and he moaned, his moans coming up from the bottom of his gut.

Jason couldn't hold back. His cock exploded into Mack's mouth just as Bob's big cock filled his ass with hot cum. After the unbelievable pleasure of being sucked and fucked, Jason collapsed on the bed.

"Hey, kid, we've got work to do," Bob stated, squeezing Jason's firm ass.

Jason slowly lifted up. "What?"

Mack had gotten into position and was waiting.

Bob asked, "What'll it be, kid, heads or tails?"

Jason looked at Bob. This was too good to be true. "Tails," he said, feeling the beginnings of a new erection.

"Thought you'd say that. Never done it before, eh, kid?"

"Nope." Jason forced the head of his cock into Mack's hole and closed his eyes. He could feel the swelling of his cock as it slid slowly into Mack's ass. Jason's cock felt much bigger inside of Mack than it had ever felt inside of any one of his girlfriends. "Oh, man," he said, as he felt his cock being squeezed by Mack's very willing chute.

"Fuck me good, Jason."

Jason forced his cock back to the edge of Mack's hole before slamming it into him again. He was glad now that he had been the first to be serviced by these guys. He knew his cock would have exploded with the first plunge into this man's ass. Jason moved with slow long strides in and out of Mack's ass.

"Fuck, kid. That's the way." Bob sucked Mack's cock deep into his throat, making gurgling noises, but nothing could be heard over Mack's loud moans and groans and screams of "Fuck my ass, kid. Suck my cock, Bob."

Jason felt his legs go weak as he shot his second load tonight into Mack's ass. "Oh, shit," Jason groaned. There was nothing like it. Mack squeezed Jason's dick as hard as he could, forcing every drop of cum out of him. Then Jason felt Mack's body tighten as he gave Bob what he was begging for.

"Got a full load for you tonight, buddy," Mack warned, just before he came.

The three men let the unbelievable feelings wash over them, and then they disentangled their glistening bodies from each other.

"Guess we gotta consider you a guest tonight now, kid. Come on."

The three men, still naked, their bodies dripping with cum and sweat got off the bed and went to the kitchen for some beer. "Pizza, Jason? On us," Mack announced, pressing the buttons on the phone.

"You bet, Mack."

The horny threesome was hungry, and the night was still young. They would need their strength. There was plenty of fucking ahead of them.

Midnight Craving

Don has no idea when it began, but he has become obsessed with men, or more specifically, a particular part of a man's anatomy. While off work due to an injury, Don begins watching porn, gay porn, and it soon begins to take over his thoughts and his dreams. Then one night when Don cannot sleep, he knows that he will not rest until he gets what he craves.

Don had never considered himself to be anything but straight. He played football in high school, a jock to the core, and he had been with more women than he could remember. Don had never ever, not even for a second, thought that he might be bi, much less gay, but over the last year or so something had changed. He had developed what could only be described as a craving for cock, a real hunger to be with a man.

It had gotten to the point recently that Don felt weird going to the gym that he had joined now that middle age was fast approaching. He had always kept himself in fairly good shape, but that didn't mean anything. Gay men weren't the only men who cared about their looks. That was a typical stereotype. Don liked to look good, and he liked to feel good about himself. But now, whenever he was in the locker room at the gym he would stare at the various guys as they undressed or after they had stepped out of the shower, when their bodies were sprinkled with water drops, their dripping tools hanging. Some of the men's cocks were soft, some were semi-solid, but some guys stepped out of the shower with rock hard erections. When Don noticed one of those guys, it was all that he could do to keep himself from running over to him and grabbing the man's hard tool that was dripping with warm water and stuffing it into his mouth.

Don's obsession with guys, or with cocks anyway, began when he was off work a few months ago with a work related injury. With nothing to do all day, Don had started surfing the Net. It wasn't difficult to stumble upon a porn site. They were everywhere. Then he happened to stumble upon a gay porn site and he watched it for awhile out of curiosity. Then he watched it for awhile longer. He seemed to be drawn to it. It was the first time that Don had watched two guys together like that, and it made him hard.

Don would lean back, make himself comfortable, and jack off while he watched the men on the screen. It was not at all unusual for Don to get hard again almost immediately after he had shot a good sized load, which was something he had never done before, or at least not since he was a teenaged boy, but he had no trouble getting a full hard-on again and again when he was watching men-on-men action. He would start watching porn earlier and earlier every day, and would watch it longer and longer with each passing day.

Sometimes Don would fantasize about the guys on the screen being with him in his own living room as he watched them do each other. "How long have I been like this?" Don asked himself this every time he watched one of these juicy porn flicks, but it didn't stop him from watching them. Don only wanted more.

Since that first time, whenever his girlfriend was over and they would watch a porn movie together, and Don would always suggest watching porn now, he would always find himself concentrating more on the men than the women, and he had no idea what the movie itself was about.

The men in porn were all so different from the guys at work. Most of the guys in porn were absolute hunks with huge thick cocks, but Don noticed one thing for certain about the guys in the films. They offered far more variety than the women. Pussy was all the same. Don would know. Before his steady girlfriend, he had been quite the player. The cocks on the screen, however, came in all sizes, varying thicknesses, and more lengths than Don could count, and to Don every one of them was mouthwatering.

The only time Don looked at the girls in movies now was when he wanted to see their facial expressions as these massive guys plowed them with their enormous tools. At first, the women looked to be in pain, but then that pain soon turned to pleasure, and they would be begging for more and more cock until their pussies were dripping with cum.

Don also loved to watch the girls suck on a guy's cock, that is, when they took their time, exploring the huge rods with their lips and their mouths until they were finally rewarded with mouthfuls of hot cream.

Don's cock ached at the thought of bringing a man to climax with his own mouth, and he dreamed of stuffing his own rod into the hungry mouth of a man, and he fantasized about it more and more.

It hadn't been all that long ago that a friend where Don worked had mentioned something about a park where guys would go cruising for other men. Don had never heard of the place, though he had lived in the city all of his life. At first, he thought his friend was full of shit. Then he wondered how his friend knew about this park. Don's friend was hot, he had to admit, and maybe his friend wanted to do him. "Shit, I've been watching way too much porn." Then the more he thought about it, about the guys cruising the park at night, the more he thought there was something sad and desperate about it, having to hide in a park just to hook up with someone. Don could not stop thinking about the park. This park that his friend talked about wasn't that far from where Don lived. "I pass by that park all the time," he said to himself. "I don't remember seeing anything."

One night, after a long day of watching his favorite porn flick, Don's curiosity and craving for cock got the better of him and he decided to go and check out the park for himself. Don was nervous as hell as he approached the park, the same park where he had played as a child, the park where he had first gone "parking" with a girl in high school, the park he passed day after day on his way to and from work, and he couldn't believe that he was parking his car in this very same park in the hope of finding some action, some guy action for himself.

Don killed the headlights and then he turned off the engine. He sat in his car and looked around. It was dark, and Don was almost afraid to get out of his car. Besides, he didn't see much of anything going on yet. A couple of guys walked by Don's car, and one of them even looked Don's way for a minute, but Don saw no one or nothing out of the ordinary. He started his car and moved to a different spot, but he still had no luck.

Something seemed to be driving him on. "What the fuck is wrong with me? I want cock. I fucking want cock." Don laughed at his own thoughts. But the more he thought about it, the more he wanted it.

Determined to get some of what he had been watching day after day at home while he pulled himself off, Don turned off his car once again and this time he got out. He walked around the park, careful not to stray too far from the safety of his car. Don looked like any other guy, and he didn't want to look suspicious, but at the same time he was definitely trying to get someone's attention. Damn, just how is it that gay guys can do this night after night?

Then, out of the corner of his eye, Don noticed train tracks that seemed to be a sort of path that led into the woods and on a whim he decided to see where it led. The tracks ended, but the path continued and was like a maze as it led Don through turn after turn. He had almost decided to turn around and head back to his car before he got completely turned around when he began to hear moans. The moans were low and soft at first. Don stopped and looked around, but he saw no one. "So now I'm hearing things," he mumbled. He moved slowly and quietly toward the moans that had begun to grow louder. He pushed his way through the tall grass and low hanging trees, not knowing what he might find.

Don stopped dead in his tracks, and then he quickly hid behind some bushes, when he saw them. Damn, this was like a scene in one of the porn flicks he had watched. There, right in front of him, was a guy on his knees, his lips wrapped around the biggest cock that Don had ever seen. The thing was so big and hard that the guy on his knees couldn't get take it all, but damn, he was going at it. The guy on his knees wasn't bad looking, either. Stripped down to just his socks, the man appeared to have what Don considered to be a rather small cock, smaller than Don's, but it was uncut and Don had only seen one of those in the adult films he had become so fond of recently.

Don tried to tear himself away from the erotic scene, but he couldn't stop watching the two men. He was drawn to them just as he was drawn to watching anything gay these days. He wanted that big heavy cock in his own mouth. Don leaned in for a closer look. He wanted to see it all, especially the huge cock that was getting a good sucking. Desperate to get a closer look, he leaned a little too far forward and lost his balance, ending up falling face first into a pile of clothes. Both men immediately stopped what they were doing and turned to look at Don.

Not seeming to be bothered by Don, the man with the enormous cock offered, "You wanna watch, or join in?" It was as easy as that. Don just stood there, his mouth hanging open. He had no idea what to do or say.

The two men grinned at each other, and then they grabbed Don. The smaller guy started stripping off Don's clothes while the man with the cock-of-all-cocks rubbed his huge rod all over Don's face, rolling it across his lips. Don had never felt another man's cock and his mouth fell open, desperately trying to catch the thing.

"You're a hungry guy, aren't you? Haven't had a big thick one for awhile?"

Don didn't answer. He held his mouth open as if waiting to be fed.

The man's fat slab of meat was covered in the shorter man's saliva, but Don didn't care. He worked the thick rod with his tongue, the way that he had imagined doing it so many times when he had jacked off to gay porn. Whatever Don was doing seemed to be working. The big man's cock grew harder and even larger in Don's mouth with every stroke of his tongue.

Don ate hungrily as he tried to take as much of the huge cock as he could. It was too big for his mouth. He gagged and choked on it, but he refused to stop.

Slowly, he got control of his breathing, relaxed his jaw, and pulled the man's cock further into his mouth. Before long, Don's nose was buried deep in this stranger's sweaty pubes. His scent was all man, and it made Don's head spin with desire.

Below Don, the smaller guy had pulled down Don's jeans and while Don tongued the massive cock, the little guy worked his tongue over Don's hairy ass.

Don gasped. It was like nothing he had ever experienced. He wanted to pull off and tell the little guy to fuck him, fuck him as hard as he could, but he didn't want to let go of the big cock in his mouth, not even for a minute. He wanted the man to shoot his manly seed into him. He felt a warm sticky sensation in the hole of his ass. It was wet, but Don could tell that it was not the man's tongue. He felt it push hard against his virgin barrier. He relaxed his ass and pushed against the thing until he felt it slide into him.

The gentle intruder was soft at first, but then it grew hard as it slid deeper inside of him. Don's body tightened when he realized that this thing was the man's cock entering him. The soft part had been the thick mushroom head, and then it became hard as the shaft made its way into him. Don was surprised, but he didn't find it painful at all. He felt only pleasure from the cock in his ass. Maybe it was good that this man wasn't all that big. Don pushed against the hard cock as the man slowly pulled out. He wanted the man to go as deeply inside of him as he could.

Don couldn't believe what was happening to him. He was getting both of his holes plugged at the same time, and he was loving every minute of it. The two men began fucking him in unison, slowly at first, and then faster and faster. Don thought they were never going to stop, and he didn't want them to stop. Then he felt it. It began in his ass, a warm sensation exploding all over his insides, coating all of him.

The grunts from the smaller guy told Don that he was shooting his load into him. The warm sensation was the man's juices coating his insides. Not long after that, the massive cock filling Don's mouth grew and then with great force it exploded full force into Don's mouth. He was getting more than a mouthful as the man blew load after load of hot sticky cum into his mouth. Don swallowed what he could of it, but much of the man's load ran down his chin and neck.

Once the two men were completely spent, they both pulled out of Don at the same time, and he fell hard onto the ground. He was drained. The cool earth beneath him felt good, but he was definitely sore. Don tried to get up but he was too drained to move. He thought he would lie there for awhile and then go back home. He thought the night was over. He thought that the two men had gone.

But Don's night had just begun. The two men turned him onto his back. Don wasn't sure that he could take any more, but he didn't have the strength to tell the men to stop. Who was he fooling? He didn't ever want the two men to stop. They were giving him exactly what his body had craved.

The smaller of the two men began working on Don's ball sac. His tongue licking all over his hairy sac made his cock spring to attention. Don was so hard he could have cum just from the man working his balls the way he was, but then his bigger friend joined him.

Beginning with Don's throbbing cock head, the big man licked the slit of Don's cock, tasting his pre-cum, searching for it, digging it out of him with the tip of his tongue. The man's mouth was hot and wet, and he took everything from Don. His tongue worked Don's cock from the head to the base. The combination of two men's mouths on him at the same time quickly brought Don to the edge. His entire body began to spasm with these new jolts of electricity bolting through him, which ended in a large explosion of cum. Blast after blast of cum poured out of Don. The big man pulled off of him and his smaller friend then covered Don's cock with his mouth, not willing to let his friend have all the fun of Don's explosion.

Don unloaded enough for both of the men and maybe even two or three more men. He didn't think he would ever stop. The two men took turns milking Don's cock until it was completely soft.

Then Don watched as the two men kissed each other, a long lover's kiss. The two men then looked at Don. The man with the huge cock said, "Glad you stopped by. Come back real soon. You know where to find us." The man winked at Don. Then the two men dressed and left Don there naked and alone in his spent and completely satisfied state.

Don lay on the ground completely naked, a little sore, but completely and blissfully spent. He thought about what had just happened to him. It had seemed more like a dream than reality. For a moment he wasn't sure what had happened. There was only one thing that he was now sure of. He would never ever be satisfied without the taste and feel of cock. This new taste of cock was only the beginning for Don. This new craving for cock was here to stay, and this park had just become his home away from home.

Husbands on the Down Low

Troy is always on the hunt for a new man, a new married man that is. On the down low for years, Troy gets from other husbands what his wife does not give him at home, and Troy gives to other married men what they desperately need. The latest of Troy's conquests is a novice in the world in which Troy is king, and Troy cannot wait to take this man to a place he has never been.

Brad and Troy first met on a Monday morning when they both reached for the same scone at their local coffee shop. "Sorry, go ahead," Brad had offered. Troy went ahead, and then he watched as Brad reached for his own scone. Troy liked what he saw.

"Where do you work?" Troy asked, as Brad was obviously dressed for an office job.

"Down the street at the tech firm."

Troy smiled, and the two men shook hands and exchanged names. Troy noticed Brad's wedding band and he held his own hand in such a way so that Brad would not miss his own band of gold. With a slight chuckle, Troy said that he might see Brad here again sometime.

"I come here every morning before work," Brad offered.

That was all that Troy needed to know about this man, for now. Troy made certain that he arrived at the coffee shop at the exact same time every morning for the next week, and every morning he saw Brad there. This soon became their morning routine, a small part of their morning routine that is. The two men began talking some each morning, the usual nothing talk, while they sipped their hot drinks. It seemed as if they instinctively began arriving a little earlier each morning and staying until they risked being late for work. Troy soon began to enjoy these mornings with Brad. He could be himself more with Brad than he could with his wife, and more than he could with any other husband. "Brad gets me," he said to himself.

Their day schedules soon began including lunch, if for no other reason than to break up the boredom of the day. Troy was an attorney, and meeting

Brad was the perfect getaway from a very stodgy and boring office. Brad admitted that he was in a rather anti-social environment himself, and this became a much needed outlet for the two men to socialize with each other.

From their first meeting, Troy knew that he wanted Brad. He wasn't sure about Brad, though. Troy could usually sense somehow if a man was like himself, on the down low, but Brad was different. "This may take awhile," he said to himself, but Troy was willing to wait. The chemistry he felt with Brad was too great not to let it take its course.

The first time the two of them did anything sexually was during the third week of their daily meetings. It was a nice day, so Troy suggested they grab a bite to eat and have lunch in the city park to enjoy the sun. Troy also knew that this was one place where the two men could be discreet. Troy knew he had to have Brad and soon. He had known it for three weeks, and he had been hard for about as long. Brad was an attractive and sexy man, and Troy was willing to do anything for him and with him that Brad desired. Troy was a few years younger than Brad, and Troy liked older men. The older the better was Troy's mantra.

Troy was willing to offer Brad what Brad's wife would never consider, and it was a temptation that Brad would be unable to resist.

"So, ready to head back?" Brad asked that day.

"Sure, but I have something to show you in my car first."

Brad was curious as they walked to Troy's car. He had parked in a somewhat secluded part of the park, and when Brad got into Troy's car, Troy got right to the point.

"I give good head and by that I mean I give great head."

Brad just stared at Troy.

"I mean it, I give the best head, and I'll bet your wife can't suck you like I can." Troy watched as Brad's dick came to life inside his pressed trousers. Then he reached over and smoothed his hand over the thickening rod. Not waiting for Brad's reply, Troy had those pressed trousers at Brad's knees and his tidy whities, too, as he licked the top of Brad's cock.

Brad was nervous, but he couldn't stop Troy if he wanted to, and he didn't want to. Troy made long strides with his tongue on and around Brad's thick pole and he could tell that Brad wasn't getting this at home. Brad began to moan and when he began squirming and throwing his head back, Troy could tell that Brad was also nervous about cumming in his mouth. Troy kept right on sucking and when Brad's gusher let loose, all he could say was, "Oh fuck," and then he was hooked. Troy could give head like nobody's business, and he could give Brad head anytime he wanted.

Afterward, Troy asked the question to which he was certain he already knew the answer. "Ever had a blowjob like that?"

"Shit, man, never. Wife won't even give it a try."

Brad was still trying to recover from Troy's mind blowing suck as he walked to his car and headed back to the office.

Troy knew that this would continue with Brad, this once a day noontime blowjob. He wondered if

Brad would tell his wife about it, or if Brad's wife would notice a difference in her husband one day. "Some do and some don't," he mumbled, responding to both of his own questions, on his way back to work.

Over the next week, Troy and Brad met for their morning coffee at the usual time, and then all they could think about as they worked at their boring jobs all morning was that they couldn't wait for lunch in the park or some other secluded area where they could be discreet. Lunch with Brad was mind blowing for both of them. Troy loved giving head to a man who never got it at home, and Brad, well, he couldn't get enough of Troy's expertise.

Troy had been doing men on the side for a long time now. Husbands were the perfect sex partners. Troy knew they would never leave their wives just as he would never leave his, so he didn't have to worry about someone becoming to clingy. It was sex, nothing more, nothing less, and married men were the best lovers. What they were not getting at home, Troy was more than happy to give them. Brad was the perfect down low man for Troy. He was a little older, never got head from his wife, and was always ready for more.

After a couple of weeks, Troy wanted to take things further. "Ever fucked a man, Brad?" They were sitting in Troy's car, before their noontime activities, and Troy had sprung the question as if he were asking Brad what he wanted for lunch.

"No," he said.

"Want to fuck me?"

Brad did, but he didn't. Troy didn't push, not yet.

"Are you ready for me, Brad?"

Brad was always ready for Troy's blowjobs. He pushed his pants down, spread his legs wide, and waited for Troy's long thick tongue and his mouth that pulled and sucked until it had taken all of Brad's thick rod. Troy sucked Brad until he was completely drained.

Then Troy began stroking himself as Brad watched. He started doing this on about their third time together, always after sucking Brad's perfect cock, hoping to entice Brad to do more. Watching another man jerk himself off was a turn-on to the married men Troy had known, and Troy had known a lot of married men. Brad thought it was erotic watching Troy pull his own hard dick. He would throw his head back and curse until he was covered in his own cum. But Troy wanted Brad to fuck him.

"You think a blowjob is mind blowing, just wait until you slide that thick slab of meat of yours inside my ass. You won't know what hit you. Better than pussy any day."

Brad was still reluctant.

On Friday of their third week together Troy asked Brad what he was doing over the weekend.

"My wife is going to her sister's, the sister who just had a baby."

"So, you're home alone all weekend?"

"Guess so," Brad admitted.

Troy's wife shopped on the weekend, every weekend, out of town. This was Troy's chance to be fucked by Brad. There was nothing like a virgin cock sliding deep inside him, and he nearly came when he thought about it. Surprisingly, it was Brad who made the suggestion. "Did you want to come over, maybe do something?"

Did he? "I'll be there tonight. See you around eight." Troy nearly came at the thought of being taken by Brad.

Troy's wife was already gone for the weekend, her usual note on the kitchen counter, when he came home that night. He showered, packed the essentials, and picked up a bottle of wine on his way to Brad's house. The two men slowly drank the wine on Brad's deck as they watched and waited for the sun to go down.

"Getting cold, better go inside," Brad said.

Troy followed, and they made a fire in the fireplace. "Come on down and sit by the fire," he urged, as he patted the floor.

Brad didn't hesitate this time. He sat beside Troy and let him put his arm around him. Brad turned to Troy, offering his lips which Troy was eager to kiss. He knew then that he would have this husband. Brad was his tonight.

"Come on, Brad. It's time." Troy took Brad by the hand and led him to the first room.

"No, down the hall," Brad said, and Troy led Brad to the end of the hall to what appeared to be a guest room. Brad liked Troy's take charge attitude in a house that he had never before been inside, and he willingly let him lead. The two men sat on the edge of the bed and this time Brad was the one who gave Troy a very passionate kiss. Troy had not expected Brad to be such an aggressor, but he gladly welcomed it. Brad slid his hand underneath Troy's shirt and began to play with his nipples. This had always been an instant turn-on for

Troy, and he gritted his teeth. Brad kissed the back of Troy's neck. It was dark, but Troy could tell that Brad was starting to take his clothes off. He then stripped Troy of his shirt and kissed him again.

The two men stripped each other of every piece of clothing and Brad pushed Troy onto the bed, spreading his body on top of him. He kissed Troy as if they were more than lovers, though both knew they could be nothing more. The emotions between them were strong as their desire for the other catapulted them over the edge of reality. Brad slid down and took Troy's hard cock into his mouth. The taste of sweat on Troy's cock was so arousing that Brad thought he would cum instantly. He took a deep breath to calm himself. Sensing that Brad might not be ready to do what Troy could not get enough of, Troy flipped him over. "Let me," he whispered.

The very sight of Brad's cock was driving him mad. He loved Brad's cock. He loved sucking it. The hardness of it, the taste and feel of it drove Troy into a sexual frenzy. "Damn, you've got a nice cock," he had said every time he sucked the thing. Troy had seen a lot of cocks and Brad's was one of the nicest cocks he had ever seen, had ever had the chance to suck, and he savored every minute of it. Troy pulled off to catch a breath and he looked into the eyes of the husband he wanted.

Brad moaned a hoarse, "Let me fuck you." Brad knew what Troy wanted and needed and after all the noontime sucks he had so eagerly given him, he wanted to give Troy the fuck he craved. They both knew what the other wanted and needed.

Troy rolled onto his back and told Brad exactly how to position himself. Troy shoved a pillow underneath him to push his ass up for Brad to enter him.

"I thought it had to be done the other way," Brad questioned.

In a hoarse whisper, Troy answered him. "You can give it to me any way you want."

Brad preferred the other way. He wasn't ready to face Troy as he fucked him. Troy rolled onto his stomach and guided Brad as he positioned the head of his cock at his lover's hole. When the first half inch of the head of Brad's cock started to push its way inside Troy, Brad leaned forward onto his hands letting his weight push the remainder of his perfect cock inside. Troy swayed his back in response to the thickness he was receiving. Brad moved slowly, not sure of this at first, and Troy moaned as each new inch of Brad entered him. He realized how much he missed a good fuck from a novice, and his body began to relax as his ecstasy began to build. Troy had not let anyone bare back him in a long time and he had forgotten how good it felt. He wanted Brad to feel like the man that he knew his wife did not make him feel. Troy wanted to make Brad feel more like a man than his wife ever could. Troy wanted to make Brad feel alive.

Troy's body had to stretch to meet the wonderful pleasing girth of Brad's cock. Every inch of his inner being was slowly being satisfied. Brad gasped and moaned as he felt the inner contours of his lover's ass as it enveloped his cock. He laid his full weight on top of Troy and began to rock back and forth. The generous amount of lube had caused the right amount of friction and with each new thrust Troy let out a small whimper. Brad kissed Troy's neck and played with his nipples as he fucked him. His gorgeous cock felt much bigger inside Troy's ass than it had inside Troy's mouth, or perhaps it had grown from the intensity of this new experience.

Brad was comfortable now and he really started to get into it. Troy knew the man had a lot of sexual tension begging to be released, just as he had during every one of their daily blowjobs.

The heat of their bodies made them both begin to sweat, and their bodies slid well over each other. Each thrust of Brad's cock was harder than the last, and it seemed as if the entire house was shaking as Brad fucked his lover. The ready pole gave Troy's prostate a thorough workout and Troy knew that he was going to explode soon. His cock was hard as it lay beneath him, and he forced it against the bed as he let out a low moan.

"Oh, shit, fuck," he cursed, and the sounds of Troy ready to cum at any moment turned Brad on even more than Troy's mind blowing blowjobs.

Brad began to fuck faster, going deeper it seemed to both men, and he fucked Troy as if it might be his last fuck ever. When Brad kissed his neck, Troy let out an abrupt "ahhh" sound and then let loose a thick stream of cum onto the bed and onto his own stomach.

Brad was close and Troy felt him tense up. Brad slid his hands underneath Troy and played with his nipples again, twisting them, pinching them, and Troy's cock let out more cum until it was drained of every drop.

Brad quickened his pace and Troy knew it would be a very short time before he exploded his seed deep inside him. When he felt Brad getting up onto his hands as if he were going to pull out, Troy squeezed the hard cock that was wedged inside of him hard, and screamed out, "Cum inside me."

Troy was breathing in short quick gasps as he waited to be filled with Brad's abundant cum. He knew how much the man stored inside of him. He had taken it every day at lunch. Brad packed a powerful load and Troy wanted it all, but this time he wanted that load inside of him.

With a few last hard thrusts, Brad came hard inside of Troy. A warm sensation filled Troy, and he felt the warm hands of Brad on his butt cheeks as Brad's first man fuck orgasm shook his entire body.

"Fuck," Brad screamed, over and over.

The man Troy had thought was a bit shy was loud now and demanding as he came inside Troy.

"Fuck, man, your ass is mine," he exclaimed, and then he finally collapsed on top of Troy, his breaths heavy on Troy's neck.

Troy could feel the cock still twitching inside of him as it pumped out its last, the few drops of cum it had left.

When Brad caught his breath, he kissed Troy's cheek and whispered in his ear, "Fuck, I needed that."

Troy knew that he did. A good man fuck was what every husband needed, according to Troy that is.

Troy breathed heavily underneath the weight of his lover. He knew that he and Brad would get together again and as often as they could. Troy was already thinking of getting their wives together and arranging for them to be out of town often. He lay there underneath Brad, a smile forming on his lips.

Mysterious Stranger

Tag's trip is boring until he comes upon a lone hitchhiker on a deserted stretch of highway. Passing him by at first, Tag turns around when he notices how sexy the man is. Too tired to drive any longer, they stop at a local hotel for the night. This is a night that Tag will not soon forget. The stranger is hungry, horny, and sexually charged. Tag has not yet been to all of the places that the erotically charged stranger has been, sexually speaking, that is.

Tag's boss rarely sent him on business trips, but this week was different. He was the chosen one, and he was bored as hell. Tag's boss was cheap and he did not believe in what he called wasting money on airplane tickets. So Tag was driving, of all things. He was driving from New York City to Minneapolis, and now he found himself somewhere on an endless highway in the middle of nowhere, it seemed. He saw truck after truck as he made his way across Ohio, and he wondered what the men in those trucks did to pass the time.

Tag was just about to doze off and had decided that it was time to look for a hotel for the night, when he noticed a man on the side of the road. The man was by himself and appeared to be hitchhiking. Tag drove on, but then he looked back. A hitchhiker, out here! It was hot tonight and Tag felt somewhat sorry for the guy being out here like he was, so he turned around and went back to offer the man a ride. Under any other circumstance, Tag probably would not have turned around. Picking up a hitchhiker was dangerous, but it was also strangely erotic to Tag. Besides, this man looked different from the hitchhikers that Tag had seen so far in his life. Maybe it was the man's tight painted on jeans that made him look too good to pass up.

Tag pulled to the side of the road and stopped the car. He could tell from the man's crotch that he was definitely a male, if Tag had had any doubt before, and the man had the body to prove it. Too good to pass this one up, Tag said to himself, no matter how dangerous the man might be.

"Where to?" he asked. Tag smiled at the man, desperately trying not to drool.

The stranger's face was the most perfect piece of patrician artwork that Tag had ever seen. He had dark black hair, jet black, and bright eyes, greenish, and he had the tan of someone who obviously spent a lot of time outdoors.

The man answered Tag's question, with a smile. "As far as you care to take me," and then he winked at Tag.

Tag was shocked and he thought he was dreaming. "Get in," he offered.

The man got in, dropped his bag in the backseat, and then sat down in the front seat. His physique was absolutely perfect, perfect for Tag, that is. The man was dressed like a cowboy, but like an urban cowboy. He didn't appear to be a man who did much manual labor, but he obviously worked out. Tag wasn't sure if the man's natural skin color was tan or if he tanned on purpose, but Tag didn't care. The man looked good. Coming out of the top of his shirt was just enough hair to run Tag's fingers through. Tag wondered if the rest of the man was as hairy as his chest seemed to be, and he hoped that he was. Oh yes, Tag wanted him. Tag wanted to feel this stranger's large hands grabbing his ass and squeezing it hard. He wanted the man's arms around him and he wanted to bury his head in the man's chest of hair.

"What's your name?" Tag asked, after introducing himself.

"The name's Jester, but I go by Jessie," he replied, not blinking an eye or smiling at Tag.

"So, why are you hitching, Jessie?"

"Just making my way across the country, Tag."

Tag glanced occasionally at Jessie who was looking at him the entire time, was practically staring at him. "Well, I've gotta stop for the night, Jessie. I'm driving in my sleep over here." Jessie did not reply, but he continued to stare at Tag.

Tag was beginning to worry that the man might be a serial killer or something, but he had gotten himself into this and now he had to see it through. He decided to stop at the nearest motel which was a bit seedy looking out here alone on this long stretch of highway.

"Well, you want to stay with me, or is this where we part ways?" Tag asked, hoping that didn't sound too weird.

Jessie's eyes lit up at Tag's invitation. "I can stay. Thanks."

Tag opened the door to the little room. It was a single room, the only kind of room that Tag's boss would spring for, and it contained only a single bed.

"I can sleep on the floor," Jessie offered.

"No, I will. You need the sleep more than I do." Tag was trying to be polite to this sexy stranger. Jessie only nodded in acceptance of Tag's offer.

"Well, I'm going to hit the shower. Make yourself at home." Tag started the shower, hoping that things would heat up between them, but so far it didn't look like that was going to happen. He was hoping that Jessie would swing open the shower door and take him right there.

Just as Tag was getting out of the shower, Jessie said to him, "Hey, Tag, got something to show you."

Tag walked out, a towel around his waist. He almost dropped the towel when he saw Jessie completely naked on the bed, smiling at him.

"Come here, Tag," he said, with a wink. Tag continued to stare. "You know you want me. I could tell right away. That *is* why you picked me up, now isn't it? You aren't so bad yourself. Now, come on over here so I can have my way with you."

Tag slowly made his way to the bed, not believing what he had just heard from this stranger. He was in shock, but how could he refuse? Isn't this what he had wanted, after all? There the man was, with a washboard for a stomach, hairy like Tag liked his men to be, and with an erection that looked like it could go all night.

Quickly drying off to keep from dripping, Tag fell into Jessie's soft fur that covered his entire body, just as Tag had hoped it would. Jessie brought his mouth to Tag's and Tag could feel the man's tongue pushing its way out to greet and enter him.

Tag was soon rolled over by Jessie, and he was now pinned underneath him. The weight of the man on top of Tag was erotically sexy and the smell of danger filled the small room. Jessie felt down along Tag's arms until he found Tag's ass and he massaged both sides with just the right amount of pressure. Then he thrust his tongue down Tag's throat with all the force that he could, and he squeezed Tag's ass as hard as he could.

Tag could feel Jessie's cock firmly pressed against his stomach, and then he felt it start to go down along his body. Jessie started licking Tag's neck and then he slid his tongue down to Tag's shoulder. He sucked and licked at every inch of Tag. His tongue swept across Tag's chest to his nipples which Jessie sucked until Tag thought that he would die right there. The pressure was too intense, almost, and just enough to make Tag want more. Tag's cock responded to the forceful nipple sucking like never before. He thrust his chest forward for the stranger, his stranger.

The man did not stop at Tag's nipples. He kept on going down along Tag's body and swirled his tongue in and around his navel. He licked into it deeper while he played with Tag's balls. Then he licked even more, harder, and then left Tag's navel and began swiping his tongue across the head of Tag's cock once or twice, teasing him into submission.

Jessie licked the slit in the head of Tag's cock that was oozing by now. He lifted Tag's cock with his tongue until it stood straight up, as if he wanted Tag to admire it, too. Slowly, he drew it into his mouth and slid it down his throat. He took all of Tag's cock easily and seductively. He didn't stop there. He continued downward and took Tag's balls into his mouth. Tag had never been taken like this.

Tag moaned. Jessie swung around and taunted Tag with his cock, swinging it over his head, lowering it to where Tag's lips were begging for it, and then he would pull it back up. Tag caught the drips that oozed from Jessie's cock as it swung just out of reach.

When Tag had been teased more than enough, he grabbed Jessie's cock and pulled it into his mouth. He was surprised at how much of it he was able to take in. Jessie had a lot to offer. Tag held it with his lips, not willing to let Jessie tease and taunt him again.

Jessie no longer was in a teasing mood. He forced his cock into Tag's mouth, fucking his face. He began shooting bursts of hot cum into Tag's throat. Tag swallowed all of it with a smile.

Jessie did not stop after that. He forced Tag's legs apart and began to eat Tag's ass. His tongue felt good inside Tag, and Jessie was soon fucking Tag's ass with his thick tongue, as he continued to fuck his face with his cock. Jessie's tongue was magical. It slid all the way in, up and down Tag's prostate, and Tag's cock was getting harder and harder.

Then Jessie stopped suddenly. "I want to fuck you," he said to Tag.

"Yes," Tag said. He would have said yes to anything that Jessie wanted at this point.

Jessie smiled, and placed the head of his massive cock into Tag's hole made ready by his expert tongue. He slowly slid all of his hard cock into Tag. Tag was going wild with his arousal. Jessie was bigger than any man Tag had ever had, and Tag was tight. Jessie was somewhat gentle, at first, and Tag soon wanted more and more. Jessie lay down on top of Tag and forced Tag's legs around him so that he could get even more of his cock inside of him.

Jessie's power was overwhelming. He was shoving his cock into Tag's ass and out of it as hard as he could now. Tag could feel the man's cock begin to quiver and he was sure that Jessie was going to explode. But he didn't. Jessie continued for what seemed like an hour, plunging deep inside of Tag, forcing himself in and then drawing back. Then it happened. The man's release inside Tag was powerful.

He shot wad after wad into him and Tag thought the man would never stop.

Jessie finally collapsed on top of Tag and began to withdraw, but Tag stopped him. "No," he said. "Keep it in all night."

The man said nothing, but he did not pull out.

Tag kissed him and drifted off to sleep with the biggest piece of man on top of him and the biggest piece of man cock inside of him.

When morning came, Tag looked at the stranger he had picked up last night. Jessie slowly awakened and began to fill Tag's ass like he had done last night. The man was good. The man knew how to fuck.

"More, Jessie," Tag demanded.

Fully awake now, Jessie gave Tag what he wanted. Tag could feel the man's entire length sliding up and down inside him. The man's tongue searched Tag's mouth and explored it again. Jessie became more demanding, more selfish, as he pleased his own hunger with Tag's body. When his cock pressed against Tag's prostate, Tag was sure that the man was going to cum immediately. But just like last night, he did not, not yet.

The man looked at Tag's cock and then he took it into his mouth, encircling the swollen head and licking it. Then he pulled all of Tag's cock into his mouth. He had complete control over Tag's cock. Tag couldn't hold back like Jessie could. He came within minutes of Jessie's expert head giving. After he had finished, the stranger licked his ass only once, teasing him again, before announcing, "I'm going to take a shower."

"Wait," Tag said. "Where will you go after today? It's not safe out there hitchhiking." Tag's body had been turned on as if Jessie had pressed a button, and he was not ready to have it turned off just yet. Jessie said nothing, but went on into the bathroom and started his shower.

The two of them left the hotel, and Jessie agreed to go with Tag for awhile. They had been driving for only about an hour when Jessie began to get horny again. He put his hand on Tag's leg.

While Tag was driving, the man slowly pulled his pants down and began to stroke him. Then he began to lick and suck Tag's cock.

"Watch it. I can't cum and drive."

"Try it. It's the most erotic thing you will ever do, almost."

Jessie slowed down to let Tag calm down, but only for a little while. Then his hot mouth slid down the shaft of Tag's cock. He slid his tongue up and down along Tag's cock until it glistened with his saliva. Tag was beginning to sweat and could barely concentrate on the road. All he could think about was this sexually charged man blowing him. Tag began to feel himself about to explode, and then he did explode, just as he parked the car at the next hotel.

Jessie sat up and covered Tag's mouth with his own, thrusting his hot tongue into Tag's mouth. They came off of each other's mouth breathless, and Tag was barely able to walk inside the hotel.

They were given the key to their room by the man at the front desk. The young man looked both of them up and down with a knowing look, and said, "If there is anything you need, I am at your service."

They thanked him and went on. They went to their room. Tag thought about what it would be like to have the young desk clerk join them in a threesome, but he didn't say anything. He wasn't sure if he was ready to share his sexy horny stranger just yet.

Inside the room, when they were alone, Jessie said to Tag, "He had a nice ass, didn't he?"

"Oh, the clerk? I guess," Tag agreed, trying to seem aloof.

Tag was dying to try it, a threesome with the desk clerk, but he didn't know what Jessie thought about it. Tag decided to let Jessie lead the way.

"Think he'd go for a threesome, Tag."

Tag shrugged his shoulders.

Jessie winked at him and said, "Come with me."

Tag followed his fearless leader back to the front desk and there he was, the gorgeous bright-eyed young man who had checked them in. He brightened up when he saw Jessie.

"Is there a problem with your room?" he asked.

"We have something to ask you," Jessie said, cutting right to the chase. "We want to know if you would come with us and show us how the showers work. We want to make sure we get it right."

Tag just stared at Jessie, impressed by his forwardness. The man smiled at Tag, and then turned his attention back to Jessie. "Yes," the young man said, with a wink. "Come with me," the man offered.

Jessie was dying to "cum" with the young man. The young man went in first and was very soon completely naked. Jessie and Tag undressed too. The young clerk then turned on the water while Tag and Jessie approached him, Jessie from the back, and Tag from the front. The three of them stepped into the shower together, and Tag and Jessie did not hesitate to help themselves to their new young man. They both wanted him. Jessie started to caress his young tight ass as Tag kissed him. The young man was aroused, but it was obvious by his first hesitations that he had never been part of a threesome before.

Tag slowly slid down the young man's chest and made his way to his cock which was fully erect, and began to suck on it. The young man was oozing already. Tag swiped his tongue across the head of the young man's cock to be the first to claim it. He held the head of the young cock in his mouth and began to suck it slowly. Jessie was pushing his cock between the man's butt cheeks and sliding it up and down.

"I'm going to cum," the young man warned.

Tag wasn't ready to let that happen, so he backed off.

The sexually charged Jessie said to Tag, "Let him take you while I take him."

Tag knew what to do. He licked the young cock and then turned around. He held the young cock, bent over a little, and pushed it into his ass. The young cock twitched a little at the new sensation.

Jessie started to fuck the young man hard which was also new to him, and it sent him almost over the edge. The young man began to rock back and forth, his cock going in and out of Tag's ass as Jessie's thrusts became more forceful. The young man took Tag's shaft in his hands as he reached around him. It wasn't long before the commanding hands of Jessie were around the young man's hands, too, and both men where holding Tag's cock.

Tag felt the young man twitch again.

He moaned. "I'm going to explode," he warned rather loudly. Tag was ready to go, too, and Jessie was also. Jessie, in charge, said, "Let's do it then."

Tag felt Jessie squeeze his cock as hard as he could and Tag's cock exploded its contents into the air. He knew that Jessie's cock was exploding its load into the young man, too. Jessie had made it known. He was not quiet in his lovemaking. The young cock soon released its load into Tag.

The three men relaxed for just a minute, and then Jessie slid down Tag's chest and began to lick up what was left of his load. He kissed Tag fully on his mouth, and then he forcefully pulled off.

The young man wanted to kiss Tag, too, and he stood up. Tag took the young mouth and forced it open with his own.

"I've never had sex like that," the young man said, breathlessly. "Let's do it again."

Jessie smiled. "Later, sweet one." Jessie and Tag left the shower to unpack in their room.

"Okay," the young clerk said as Jessie and Tag walked away, and he went back to his job.

"You serious, Jessie? Tonight?"

"Why the fuck not? The kid wants it."

Tag knew it was true. He had finally met someone who was as horny as he. "You're right," he said.

Jessie smiled. Then he covered Tag's mouth with his and he kissed him hard. "Trust me, Tag. We are going to have fun tonight."

Tag had dozed off for awhile and he thought he had been dreaming, but when he woke up he looked down and saw his cock buried inside Jessie's mouth. He was sucking him hard. Tag came almost immediately at the sight of this erotic action in his half awake, half asleep state. "Damn," he said. "I thought it was a dream."

Jessie smiled and licked his lips. They slept again in each other's arms, not caring when they woke up.

Sneaking Out

Sam has a boyfriend, and Sam considers himself to be a pretty good boyfriend to his boyfriend. But at night, at night when his boyfriend is sleeping, Sam gets so horny sometimes that he cannot stand it. It is during these times that Sam goes to a special place in the woods, a place that only cheaters know about.

Sam was a pretty good boyfriend, or at least he thought he was. But sometimes, in the darkness of night, he would get really horny. His current boyfriend was pretty straight-laced, but very good to have around in certain social circles. He had done a lot for Sam's career. Sam really didn't want Mathew to know about his secret. But on those nights when Sam got really horny, he would sneak out very quietly, making sure not to wake Mathew. He would head out to the deep woods behind the very spacious ranch that Mathew had purchased for them. There was a place in the trees about two miles from where they lived, and Sam would run as fast as he could to get there. In this very special place nestled in the trees was a log cabin that many lovers frequented, lovers who were cheaters, that is.

Tonight Sam was almost there, out of breath as usual. He turned onto the secluded little road that was the last stretch to the little cabin and followed it to its final destination. No one was there, yet, but it was early. Winded, Sam sat down on the sofa and relaxed. Not realizing it, he dozed off for awhile.

The next thing he knew he was staring at a cock that was just there in front of him. He moved his eyes upward until they met those of a young man about his same age.

"What's your name?" the man asked.

"It's Sam, and I don't remember you being here before."

The man sat down next to Sam naked, and he turned to him. "I'm Blue. Of course, that's a nickname, but that's all you get."

Sam was intrigued by this man who called himself Blue. He did look good. He had clear skin, with nice hair, but Sam's eyes seemed to focus on the man's cock.

"Here," Blue said, and handed Sam a beer. Sam wasn't much of a beer drinker, but he thought, why not? He took the beer and it really wasn't that bad. He kept looking at the man's cock and the longer he looked at it, the more he wanted it. He was always horniest late at night when Mathew was sleeping.

Making no excuses for being forward, Blue reached over and put his hand on Sam's cock. "Better let that thing breathe, Sam," he said, and looked at Sam with his bedroom eyes. "Here, I'll help save the poor thing," Blue said, and he had Sam naked from the waist down before he knew it.

Blue was a big man and with one movement he lifted Sam up and placed him onto his lap. "That's much better," he said, running his hand along Sam's cock.

Sam closed his eyes. This was why he came here late at night. He drank the rest of his beer, and then he leaned down to kiss Blue. Blue kissed him back, but just briefly. He lifted Sam up until Sam was resting on the top of the sofa.

"Feed me that thing I just freed," he demanded.

Sam didn't have to do a thing. Blue's hands were on his ass, forcing Sam's cock into his mouth, as Sam held onto Blue's head and to the back of the sofa.

Blue began to run his hands over Sam's ass once he had Sam's cock firmly inside his mouth. He lightly stroked Sam's ass crack. His movements were slow at first and it felt good. "Sam, your ass feels good to the touch. Better than most."

The next thing Sam felt was a finger probing his asshole. Blue continued to feed himself Sam's cock, and soon he was shoving two fingers into Sam's hole. Sam tried to move against Blue's hand to get even more inside him. Blue got the hint and soon he had three fingers in Sam's hole, and it felt even better.

"Damn, Blue," Sam moaned, "You are making me so hot."

As Blue sucked harder and faster and probed even deeper, Sam began to warn him. "Get ready for a blast," Sam warned.

Blue could feel Sam's cock head swell, and then the warm cum blasted down his throat. He took every drop and then squeezed the tender head to try to get even more.

"Uh," Sam groaned.

Blue continued to hold Sam's cock in his mouth as it got a little softer and smaller. "Sam, my boy, you are the best," he said, and he plopped Sam back down onto the sofa beside him.

Sam was panting just like before when he was running to get here. He looked over at Blue who was stroking his own cock.

"Mm, I like this. You want to stroke me, Sam?"

Sam took the hard cock in his hand and began to stroke it. Blue laid his head back and let Sam do whatever he wanted. He climbed onto Blue's lap again and placed the cock where he had felt it teasing his hole before.

Blue began to play with Sam's ass again, feeling his cock as it slid inside Sam. Blue withdrew his finger and pushed Sam down hard on his cock.

"Uh," Sam moaned.

"Nice, huh?" Blue bragged.

"Oh, yes," Sam agreed.

The man was hot, and Sam was horny. Blue grabbed Sam's hips and held on so tight that Sam could barely move. Sam didn't have to do a thing. Blue took total control again and he lifted Sam up and down onto his cock. It felt so good that Sam began to move with him. He thought that he could feel Blue getting close, so he slowed a bit, but Blue was stronger and he kept up his pace.

Sam was being slid up and down the man's solid rod. Each stroke was longer and more pleasurable than the previous one, and Sam was totally at Blue's mercy. The big hands were kneading Sam's ass.

Sam soon felt Blue's cock filling up for the big finale and his warm cum began to rise from his balls. Then he felt the strong forceful bursts from Blue spurting forth into his hole, filling him completely. Sam wanted him to keep going forever but eventually, Blue pumped himself dry, and Sam was full to overflowing.

Panting once again, Sam was soon lifted up and off of Blue again and plopped down onto the sofa again. They both lay back and rested for awhile. They waited for the other to say or do something first. Sam knew he should be getting home, but he didn't know if he had the strength for the two mile stretch.

Blue reached over and urged Sam's cock to hardness once again and Sam couldn't resist. He was hot and horny again. He got down onto the floor on all fours, offering his open ass to his hot lover.

"You want it, baby, you got it," Blue said, and he got down on the floor behind him.

Sam was ready for Blue to take him doggie style. Blue slipped right in, and Sam's pleasurable moans grew louder and louder as this hot lover thrust in and out of his hole. When Sam felt the man's pubic hairs brushing against him, he thrust himself backward, and Blue held his hips and pumped him hard. Blue soon let another burst fill Sam just as Sam sprayed the floor of the little cabin.

"Man, that felt good."

"Mm, mm," Blue moaned, as he squeezed Sam's ass. "We've got to do this again, and often."

Blue collapsed on Sam, nearly flattening him, until Sam had regained enough strength for the long walk home.

Two Loves

I dreamed I stood upon a little hill,
And at my feet there lay a ground, that seemed
Like a waste garden, flowering at its will
With buds and blossoms. There were pools that
dreamed
Black and unruffled; there were white lilies
A few, and crocuses, and violets
Purple or pale, snake-like fritillaries
Scarce seen for the rank grass, and through green nets
Blue eyes of shy peryenche winked in the sun.
And there were curious flowers, before unknown,
Flowers that were stained with moonlight, or with
shades
Of Nature's willful moods; and here a one
That had drunk in the transitory tone
Of one brief moment in a sunset; blades
Of grass that in an hundred springs had been
Slowly but exquisitely nurtured by the stars,
And watered with the scented dew long cupped
In lilies, that for rays of sun had seen
Only God's glory, for never a sunrise mars
The luminous air of Heaven. Beyond, abrupt,
A grey stone wall. o'ergrown with velvet moss
Uprose; and gazing I stood long, all mazed
To see a place so strange, so sweet, so fair.
And as I stood and marvelled, lo! across
The garden came a youth; one hand he raised
To shield him from the sun, his wind-tossed hair
Was twined with flowers, and in his hand he bore
A purple bunch of bursting grapes, his eyes

Were clear as crystal, naked all was he,
White as the snow on pathless mountains frore,
Red were his lips as red wine-spilith that dyes
A marble floor, his brow chalcedony.
And he came near me, with his lips uncurled
And kind, and caught my hand and kissed my mouth,
And gave me grapes to eat, and said, 'Sweet friend,
Come I will show thee shadows of the world
And images of life. See from the South
Comes the pale pageant that hath never an end.'
And lo! within the garden of my dream
I saw two walking on a shining plain
Of golden light. The one did joyous seem
And fair and blooming, and a sweet refrain
Came from his lips; he sang of pretty maids
And joyous love of comely girl and boy,
His eyes were bright, and 'mid the dancing blades
Of golden grass his feet did trip for joy;
And in his hand he held an ivory lute
With strings of gold that were as maidens' hair,
And sang with voice as tuneful as a flute,
And round his neck three chains of roses were.
But he that was his comrade walked aside;
He was full sad and sweet, and his large eyes
Were strange with wondrous brightness, staring wide
With gazing; and he sighed with many sighs
That moved me, and his cheeks were wan and white
Like pallid lilies, and his lips were red
Like poppies, and his hands he clenched tight,
And yet again unclenched, and his head
Was wreathed with moon-flowers pale as lips of death.
A purple robe he wore, o'erwrought in gold
With the device of a great snake, whose breath

B.J. Scott   108

Was fiery flame: which when I did behold
I fell a-weeping, and I cried, 'Sweet youth,
Tell me why, sad and sighing, thou dost rove
These pleasent realms? I pray thee speak me sooth
What is thy name?' He said, 'My name is Love.'
Then straight the first did turn himself to me
And cried, 'He lieth, for his name is Shame,
But I am Love, and I was wont to be
Alone in this fair garden, till he came
Unasked by night; I am true Love, I fill
The hearts of boy and girl with mutual flame.'
Then sighing, said the other, 'Have thy will,
I am the love that dare not speak its name.'

~Lord Alfred Douglas~

The Road Not Taken

Two roads diverged in a yellow wood,
And sorry I could not travel both
And be one traveller, long I stood
And looked down one as far as I could
To where it bent in the undergrowth;

Then took the other, as just as fair,
And having perhaps the better claim,
Because it was grassy and wanted wear;
Though as for that the passing there
Had worn them really about the same,

And both that morning equally lay
In leaves no step had trodden black.
Oh, I kept the first for another day!
Yet knowing how way leads on to way,
I doubted if I should ever come back.

I shall be telling this with a sigh
Somewhere ages and ages hence:
Two roads diverged in a wood, and I--
I took the one less traveled by,
And that has made all the difference.

~Robert Frost~

Stopping By Woods on a Snowy Evening

Whose woods these are I think I know.
His house is in the village though;
He will not see me stopping here
To watch his woods fill up with snow.

My little horse must think it queer
To stop without a farmhouse near
Between the woods and frozen lake
The darkest evening of the year.

He gives his harness bells a shake
To ask if there is some mistake.
The only other sound's the sweep
Of easy wind and downy flake.

The woods are lovely, dark and deep.
But I have promises to keep,
And miles to go before I sleep,
And miles to go before I sleep.

~Robert Frost~

The contents of this book constitute a work of fiction. All events, themes, persons, characters, and plots are fictional inventions of the author. Any resemblance and/or reference to actual events, as well as to any persons living, deceased, or yet to be born is purely coincidental and entirely unintentional.

No part of this book may be reproduced or transmitted in any form or by any means, graphic, electronic, or mechanical, including photocopying, recording, taping, or by any information storage retrieval system, without the permission in writing from the author and publisher.

Beau to Beau Books
Celebrations of Male Love
E-mail: info@beautobeau.com
Website: http://www.beautobeau.com

Printed in the United States of America
For additional copies, please e-mail us at
info@beautobeau.com

Beau to Beau Books in Print

Panda Heart
Black Diamond
ER Knights
Maestro and Me
A Grand Illusion
If You Just Smile
Cowboy Coarse; Branding Dylan
Along Came Two and Along Came You
A Time For Us
The Haunting of Quentin
Fine Things
The Doctor's Secret
Desire Ordained
BunBun
He Came With a Rose
Trey's Daddies
Bear Hugs
Money Maker
Fun With S&M
More Fun With S&M
Hot Erotic Nights
Hot and Hung
Blood Scent
A Man For All Seasons
I Kissed a Man

Especially for Young Adults

Harvest Grove
First Born
Super Star
Haven at Harvey Milk High
and then, he Kissed Me

More Books in Print Coming Soon. To read excerpts of any of the Beau to Beau books, in print or ebooks, please feel free to visit the Beau to Beau website, **http://www.beautobeau.com.**

The stories in this print book, as well as additional Beau to Beau Books, are available in ebook form from the following:

Apple iBookstores

Barnes & Noble

Amazon Kindle Stores

Rainbow ebooks

All Romance ebooks

1 Place for Romance

Bookstrand

3353454R00063

Printed in Great Britain
by Amazon.co.uk, Ltd.,
Marston Gate.